THE OLD MAN OF THE BLACK

A Christmas Ghost Story

STEVE GRIFFIN

Copyright Steve Griffin 2025

All rights reserved. No part of this publication may be reproduced, stored in a retrieval system, or transmitted in any form or by any means, electronic, mechanical, photocopying, recording or otherwise, without the written permission of the publisher.

by Steve Griffin

The Ghosts of Alice:
The Boy in the Burgundy Hood
The Girl in the Ivory Dress
Alice and the Devil
Alice and the Broken Dead
The Woman in the Widow's Lace

Christmas Ghost Stories:
Black Beacon
The Old Man of the Black

Psychological Thriller:
The Man in the Woods

The Secret of the Tirthas (young adult):
The City of Light
The Book of Life
The Dreamer Falls
The Lady in the Moon Moth Mask
The Unknown Realms
Swift: The Story of a Witch *(prequel)*

I.

The Snowstorm

1.

There were places they didn't deliver to, which Ryan wished they did – and others they did, that he wished they didn't.

This was one of those.

But here he was, late, checking the satnav, 4.48, the day before Christmas Eve, listening to Chris Rea, *Driving Home For Christmas*, on his way to the final drop-off, deep in the countryside.

And boy, was the weather bad. Appalling – treacherous, even. The snow had started on Tuesday, after his eleven o'clock drop to Madge Taylor, up at Braecluain. She'd warned him to put his snow chains on then and there, but he knew the Toyota, its grip was good and could cope with a fair bit of weather. He'd made it through the rest of the day, with only one little skid coming down the mountain road. But the snow hadn't stopped. It just kept coming, thick, amorphous lumps of greyish white, making the fields look like rough, frothing sea.

From the delivery point of view, it was a nightmare. Up until now, the festive season had been mild, just a few rainy days with sunny, even warm, patches in between. He'd been in a T-shirt half the time, not even noticing the cold. No more. Spring to winter in a day, that was Scotland. The land was now encrusted, the roads icy and perilous. And tonight – tonight it was sleeting, a strong wind coming from the west. The spindly black branches of hawthorns and oaks raking the road at the edge of his headlights. Tonight was a bad, bad night.

And he still had this one delivery to make. He checked the sheet he'd printed, crunched up, folded. Rose Leslie, Mrs – Ashcraig Grange, Drummore. A nice name, Rose Leslie. He would be there in – he checked the satnav – eight minutes – and then it was back, back to Newton in time for a quick shower then beers with Dylan and Rob down the Two Dogs. A nice, warm, cheery pub with his mates. Yes, home by six, if he was quick.

The white road dipped in the yellowish glare of the headlights and he pressed the brake, not too hard to cause a slide.

He peered ahead, silencing the music and hearing the clunk of the wipers now the engine was quiet. It didn't just dip, the road – it vanished. 1 in 5, at least. And covered in snow, packed into ice in the tyre channels. No way would he make it.

He looked at the map, reassuringly bright and clear, flipped since half two into blue-grey night light.

It wasn't too long a stretch, you could be sure – almost – by the way the road swerved soon after the dip. The satnav was good on the Toyota, but he wished he'd invested in a Garmin with a gradient facility, you needed one on some of these more remote Highland roads. What could he do?

He inched forwards, into the splatting sleet. Pulled up the handbrake, opened the cabin door.

The wind whipped away the built-up heat, lashed his face with hail like grit. He lunged across the passenger seat, grabbed his waterproof, tugged it on quickly and pulled down the hood. Reached back in and released the glove compartment, took out his torch. He flicked it on and trod out through the snow in his Docs.

OK, so the road descended sharply for ten metres or so, before twisting away right into a shallower curve.

Presumably beyond that, it was a gentler incline, all the way down to the valley floor, where the house, Ashcraig, lay. On its own, not in a hamlet or anything. There were trees fringing the road, snow banked on the sides into smaller, thorny scrub, as far as he could see with his torch, through the blizzardous dark. Jeez, it was freezing. The sleet stung his cheeks.

He walked back and opened the door, stepped up swiftly and sat himself back in front of the wheel. Slammed the door. Switched off the torch and felt the numbness already settled in his red fingers. He wiped away the ice thawing on his brow and turned the fan on full to feel the heat blast his hands and face.

What was he going to do?

He knew what he *should* do. What any sane person would do. Go back. There was no point in risking this road in this weather. More likely than not, he'd end up in a ditch – or worse. No, he should definitely reverse up to the nearest passing place, pull a U-turn, and go home.

That's what he should do.

But this was a new customer of Fresh & Friendly, the eco food delivery business he'd started with Isla just over eighteen months ago. What would *she* say? What would Isla say now?

He knew what she would say. With a cheeky grin and a wink, she'd tell him he couldn't let Mrs Rose Leslie down. Not at Christmas. How *un*-friendly would that be? Not at all in keeping with company values…

And besides, it wasn't like they'd been creaming it in. Last year, they'd invested in a new driver, a fresh-faced kid called Harvey, but within six months they'd had to lay him off and return to doing all the driving themselves. On top of their existing base, they now needed to add at least a dozen new customers a quarter to reach this year's target, to pay off the loans and have a little bit extra to live. Or, at least, *he* did.

Go. He would go.

Ryan turned up the stereo – it was Mariah Carey now, wasn't it always? – eased down the handbrake, and put the Toyota into gear.

2.

At the bottom of the hill he stopped and leaned forward across the wheel, breathing out.

It had been a close thing at one stage, he'd felt that slipping-on-air thing on one of the corners, but – he'd made it. He thought of a cigarette, an imagined nano-second of nicotine hit – then remembered he'd given up. Stopped. Hadn't had one since Bella. No more cigarettes for you, Harris.

His problems weren't over. The road, sheltered in the valley, was piled high with fresh snowfall, making his journey edgy and slow. He started off again, revving, braking, steering into the mini-skids, easing the truck back gently on to the centre of the track. He peered close to the windscreen to see through the dark and sleet. Trees, oaks, birch, continued to overhang the road, sagging with their burden of snow and ice. There were gaps where he saw through to open fields. But there was no way of seeing the mountain that rose to his left, the hills further off to his right. Too dark, too obstructed by this godawful pounding from the heavens.

He laughed. At least they were getting a white Christmas. Then felt a shadow. At least *he* was getting a white Christmas.

If he ever managed to get back up that hill.

3.

He was further down the track, just two minutes away from Ashcraig, he'd be seeing it soon – when something thumped against his driver's side window.

He glanced sideways and – what the hell? – saw someone at the side of the road.

Someone in a place where the scrub thinned, was that a gate into a field beyond?

Someone who wasn't anyone, because there was no one there. No one he could see, anyway. They'd gone.

Ryan stopped the van, switched off the news, depressing stuff of multi-car pile ups caused by the weather, one in the far north, the other closer to home on the A82, the stretch between Dumbarton and Glasgow.

He looked again, but it was all grizzled sleet to the side of the vehicle, poorly lit in the margin of the headlights. But he'd seen someone, he was sure. A slight figure in a coat, their arm swinging down, strangely clear amid an unusually deep blackness. As if…

He changed his focus, the verge blurred as he looked at the window itself. There, despite the sludge of the weather, he could see it – a small, cleared, wet space, a dribbling circle of crystals at its edge. Like…

A snowball.

Like someone had chucked a snowball at him, in his van.

4.

Still in the damp waterproof, he picked up the torch and flung open the door.

'Hello!' he called, jumping down into crunching powder. His voice was snatched by the wind, the crazy whistle and clack of branches all around him. Bitten by the chill, he swore.

'Look, if there's anyone there, there's a lift on offer back to the house…' he shouted. He guessed if there was anyone there, they could *only* have come from the house. Where else was there?

'You'd be wise to take me up on it, in this bloody *dreich*,' he added.

He advanced into the deeper fall at the verge. Stepped up on to the bank, shone the torch around. A few spikes of sedge pushed through the crust, the sign of damp ground. He'd been right, there was a farm gate back there between the trees, giving on to an open, grey, dismal field.

There was no one there.

'What the…' Ryan muttered to himself, tugging his hood down to protect his eyes. 'I'm not hanging around,' he said loudly. 'I've got to get a drop off done, so's I can be home before this…'

He stopped. What point, talking to the thin air? Or rather, the thick air, thick with this treacherous sleet. He shone the torch around one more time, into the tangle of the near blackthorn, across tree trunks, creased and black and greenish with wet and moss, over the gate, casting an elongated shadow of bars over the snow beyond. Should he check behind the gate? What if there was someone there, cold or injured, someone who'd chucked a snowball to try and catch his attention. Someone who needed help?

It didn't make sense. Lifting his legs high, he stepped carefully up the bank, put his boot down in the sedge for firm footing, made his way to the gate. Leaned on it, peered left and right, shining the torch along the hedge bank, the old, shuddering bramble and tattered grasses that struggled up through the smothering snow.

Nothing. There was no one there.

'Bugger this.' He turned and marched back towards the van, stumbling and almost falling in the snow when the bank finished more abruptly than he'd expected.

But as he opened the door and raised his boot to the step he turned once again and shone his torch toward the gate.

'I'm going now,' he yelled, loud as he could. The wind moaned back at him, like some cruddy movie, sifting through the wild canopy.

He shook his head and climbed back into the warmth and stillness of the cab. Slammed the door. Took off the handbrake and looked back at the window. The mark of the snowball – if that's what it was, not just a lump of ice falling from a branch overhead – was gone now, blown away by the wind, overtaken by the blast of fresh sleet. He began to rev, to drive off slowly, glancing to both sides as he went.

He was certain he'd glimpsed somebody there, at the side of the road.

A small figure, chucking something at the van.

5.

'Jesus, Mary, Joseph and the wee donkey…' he said under his breath, mimicking the Northern Irish police inspector from the TV show.

He slowed the van to a halt as he emerged from an avenue of trees and the house, Ashcraig Grange, came into sight.

House? More like a bloody castle! Or at least one of those huge, Highland Laird country manors from the nineteenth century. Built from grim granite, Ashcraig had a square footprint based around a large open courtyard. At the front, its two wings were connected by a long wall pierced by a portcullis gate – at the back was surely the main residence, but it was too far away in the snow-swirling courtyard to see. Ryan noticed the risen prongs of the portcullis near the top of the archway, but suspected it was mainly for show. The righthand, eastern wing was fronted by a square tower, its top some fifty or sixty foot up in the driving blizzard. The tower had narrow set of windows down the middle, partially obscured by a full-grown Scots pine. The left wing had an enormous, pitched roof with a giant chimney, two generous stories tall; rectangular latticed windows, the outermost aglow with winey light, pierced the heavy wall. Another shaggy, conical pine grew towards the western edge, almost reaching the parapet of the long entrance wall.

For a moment, seeing the pines in grey snow, Ryan was lifted from the struggle of the journey. He felt a shiver of joy, a connection made with pines from long ago, a scene from childhood, at Christmas, he couldn't remember when – but it touched something rich, indelible in his soul.

'Like something out of Disney…' he muttered, accelerating forward on the gravel, somehow still clear in places from the snow. He glanced at the delivery sheet again, wondering if there were instructions about where he was supposed to go. To the front door, like a normal house? Presumably ahead, through the portcullis? Or was there a side, or back, entrance, one for the *lower classes*? He thought of Downton Abbey, somewhere to keep the base functioning of the place out of sight of entitled owners...

Ryan chuckled. Look at him, talking himself into fantasies. Sure, the house was big. But it wasn't ridiculously big. Mr and Mrs Leslie were probably just some couple who'd made a bit of money thirty years ago, perhaps with a tech startup, bought an old rundown place like this before property prices went completely silly. They probably didn't even have a servant – did you call them servants these days, or was it better to say maid, or cook? You could look after a place like this on your own, he was sure. Put the hoover round every other week, stagger the dusting. Jeez, at least the first impressions of the place were keeping his spirits up.

He drove the Toyota through the gateway into the forecourt.

Even though the snow still whirled, he could immediately sense the relative shelter. Little eddies of leaves, squalls of ice, still blew about, but the exposure was diminished. He was pleased, he would prefer not to get utterly drenched and frozen unloading the Christmas Day victuals, ham, turkey from a farm only ten miles away, the King Edwards, leeks, parsnips, a two-year pudding, and so on. The main door, squat and reinforced, was straight ahead, more buttery, diamond-paned windows running away to either side. To his right, the bulkier, taller wing with the tower had two more doors giving on to the courtyard. Left, there were smaller windows on the second floor but the whole of the floor below was given over to a huge car port, stone pillars dividing three sets of garage doors. The middle set was open; Ryan could see a black SUV, a Range Rover, parked in there.

'Clearly not short of a penny or two,' he said, whistling and easing the Toyota across the snow-covered cobbles to stop at the steps to the main door.

He switched off the engine, then the stereo, silencing something more modern, Spector-esque, Home for the Holidays by Emmy the Great, the one with that guy from Ash.

For a millisecond, it felt like hush, with the engine and music gone. But then the drone of the wind, the clatter of ice on the bonnet, came through into the insulated cabin. Ryan forced down a sudden desire to remain in the cabin, in the warmth and comfort. He needed to hurry, to get the food dropped and be back on his way before it all became too treacherous. He opened the door and stepped down into the snow. Like in Good King Wenceslas, he followed a set of footprints that hadn't quite been covered by the recent fall up to the giant, bar strapped door. Reaching into the middle of a holly and ivy wreath, he rapped the black knocker.

And waited, for an occupant of Ashcraig to answer.

6.

After a while, probably not a minute – time passed ice-slow in this weather – he knocked again.

He turned about, looking past the Toyota at the forecourt, the mostly dark windows with their white ledges, the giant tower with its parapets also lined with snow, high up in the flurry of the sky. Despite the few windows with light – or at least half-light, from table lamps or possibly candles – the place seemed oddly quiet. He began to worry. Were they out? Gone to dine with friends, or in the pub of some local village, eating out one last time before entering the strange cocoon of the days around Christmas? Had they forgotten they'd made a food order from the Vale of Leven's finest green delivery service? Earthy Good Quality, with a Scots Smile. No, that was terrible! Eighteen months, and they still hadn't got their strapline right…

Shit, was he cold!

He reached in his pocket for his phone to call the contact number. There was a possibility they wouldn't hear the door in a place this size. Perhaps they were all in some family room halfway up the second-floor wing, playing Twister or Sardines something…

Damn, the phone was still in the cab. He trudged down the steps, seeing the crushed-up mess of the snow where his own, hefty prints had landed amid the faded others, pulled open the door, and shut himself in again. Grabbed the phone from the passenger seat and dialled the number on the sheet, hoping his single bar of reception would hold.

As the phone burred, he checked the time on the dashboard. Five-twenty-five. He watched the front door, praying it would open.

'Come on…'

There was a match on, ice hockey, the Dundee Stars vs. Sheffield Steelers, at seven. He'd been hoping to catch some of it before the pub. Fat chance. Couldn't watch it on catchup, either, only live…

After a minute of ringing he ended the call. He breathed out heavily. Should he try another of the doors? He felt a rising sense of frustration, verging on anger. Didn't they realise how much it took to get this food to them, in this weather? Were they that…?

He saw something move, a blurring of light in one of the windows on the second floor, just to the right above the main door. He leaned forward and peered up to get a better look. A child, a teenage girl with long hair, in a dress, was there, one of her palms against the latticed windowpane.

So there was someone in! He jumped out of the van and looked up, preparing to signal to her. But when he looked again she'd vanished. He heard a heavy clunk and looked back at the entrance.

Slowly, the great door of Ashcraig began to open.

7.

'Uh… it's your delivery? Fresh and Friendly?'

He tried to shelter in the recessed doorway, without seeming too forward.

The person – a woman – in the shadowy interior said something. All he could see was one side of her pallid face, a mass of dark hair.

'Sorry – it's blowing a gale out here,' he said, grimacing. 'Any chance I could step inside for a minute? So you can tell me where you'd like it?'

'…sure…'

He still couldn't hear her, her voice was too soft. It might be rude but he advanced a little, stepping over the threshold, thinking, it's vampires need to be invited in, isn't it? But he hadn't come all this way to mess around.

His confidence worked. The woman opened the door a little further, giving him the space to step around it, into the surprising warmth – cosiness, even – of the interior. There was a big, beautiful Christmas tree standing by the door, glowing with golden bands of fairy light and hung with decorations that looked homemade, tied cinnamon, paper angels, that kind of thing. He smelt the fresh, piney scent.

'Mrs Leslie?' he said.

She pushed the door to, stood straight in front of him. She was a tall woman, with white skin and long, dark brown hair, wearing a full-length pleated dress. Flowery, dark green.

'Who are you, again?' she said.

Edinburgh, he thought. The accent, barely sounding Scottish at all. Posh. Edinburgh, for sure, or somewhere from the Borders.

'I'm Ryan Harris,' he said, lifting a hand. She stared at it until he let it fall back to his side. 'From Fresh and Friendly. I've got your Christmas order in the van, all the trimmings. You're going to have a fantastic few days, you wait until you taste John Fenning's ham cut…'

Her mouth was open. It was a wide mouth, her lips pale pink, creased. Her teeth were white, one or two slightly crooked at the bottom. Possibly a little stained, although it was hard to tell in the soft lighting, just the tree, a standing lamp with an ochre shade, and a small table lamp by the door. She stared at him until he began to wonder, what was the matter?

'Your food order,' he said, thinking he might not have explained himself properly. 'Rose Leslie, Ashcraig Grange, Drummore, FK17, four-thirty on Wednesday 23rd? I'm from the company you ordered from, Fresh and Friendly.'

Her lips twitched up, her eyes, green, almost gem-like, blazed. 'Of course,' she said. 'I'm so sorry. Fresh and Friendly. Yes. I thought… when I saw the van, I thought you might be someone else. Someone lost in the storm. I think the bad weather… I suppose, I'd written you off, subconsciously, at least, thought you wouldn't be coming.'

What a strange thing to say, he thought. Subconsciously. 'We wouldn't want to leave a customer high and dry the day before Christmas Eve,' he said, summoning all his charm into his warmest smile. He had a good smile, he knew, everyone loved his grin. Twinkly, Isla said.

The woman's face fell. She looked left, and he followed her gaze, taking in more of their surroundings. They were in a long, wide foyer, with double doors ahead leading to a dining room – he could see the table laid – and doors to the left and right. The one to the right was open, and beyond was a large living room with sofas and an open fire, tinsel and cards over the mantelpiece and another glowing tree.

'Do you mind taking them to the kitchen for me?' she said. 'Through those doors on the left, then first right.'

'Not at all. Would you like me to unpack them for you?'

She raised a finger to her lips, frowned. Clearly not of a mind to make decisions tonight, thought Ryan. He wondered if she was having a hard time, perhaps she'd been caught up in the weather earlier, too.

She nodded, with a small smile.

He turned about and swung back the door. 'Five minutes and I'll leave you to yourselves,' he said.

'…selves…' he heard her say, her voice lost in the wind as he stomped back into the freeze.

8.

'Where do you want these?'

He knew she was hovering, through the double doors from the kitchen to the dining room, where he glimpsed a second fire. There was music playing from a smart speaker by the bread bin, something quiet and classical. He'd already unloaded the chilled stuff into the tall fridge on the far wall, the hulking great turkey and ham from John's farm, the leeks, parsnips, carrots, creams and premade packet gravies, but he didn't want to go rummaging for the right cupboards for the dry goods, the beans and sardines and snacks.

She came in, moved up to the granite island, the longest he'd ever seen. 'Just in the food cupboard,' she said, gesturing to the units on the interior wall, with their under-cupboard lighting.

'Here?' he opened a chest height pine door, saw plates and bowls.

'That one,' she said, pointing.

The next was full of tinned food. 'OK,' he said, leaning over the wooden crate and lifting the cans up on to the shelves.

'Don't worry,' she said. 'I'll do the rest. Now you've got the heavy stuff away?' It sounded like a question.

'Sure,' he said. Then remembered the bubbly. He stooped and lifted it from amid the bottles of claret. 'For you and Mr Leslie,' he said, brandishing the label at her. 'A special Christmas gift, from us.' They could scarcely afford the free champagne, but Isla had insisted last year, a quality, free gift for each new customer. Cement the relationship, she'd said. Loss leader, she'd said, as he'd rolled his eyes.

The woman stared at the label. 'That's – that's lovely,' she said.

'Shall I pop it in the fridge? Be nice and cold for Christmas Day.'

'Thank you,' she said.

9.

Back on the road, he tried calling Rob.

The silence was palpable, seemed to throb as he glanced between the bowing sleet and the blank call screen on his satnav. After a few seconds there was a faint bleat as the call dropped out.

'Bugger,' he said. His reception was gone. Hardly surprising.

Sleigh Ride by the Ronettes returned in force, making him pat away at the wheel. He dropped down the wiper speed a notch, as the snow began to ease. The van was making reasonable progress, but he knew what was still to come… the hill.

It was a shame he couldn't get through to Rob. He fancied chatting, he was a bit hyper after this afternoon, the weather, Ashcraig, the weird snowball incident and the slightly odd Mrs Leslie, fey, that's the word for her, wasn't it, she was definitely fey. Flighty?

He wondered what Isla would call her. Dizzy. He heard her saying it, her West coast lilt, felt a pang.

He thought about Mrs Leslie. That pre-Raphaelite look, the dark, wavy hair, wan complexion, those broad, pink lips. Her eyes, green, starry, he'd noticed in the better light of the kitchen. She had a quality about her. Mr Leslie, whoever he was, was a lucky man.

She was a looker, for certain, and… dizzy.

Ronnie's vocals fizzled, distorted, and then were entirely erased as the frequency broke.

'…inging…' they came in, then fuzzed out again. He turned the volume down to nothing.

He still had forty minutes until he was home. And, of course, the hill, which he could see now emerging between the black, bent trees. The good thing was that the snow was easing.

He'd be alright.

10.

He switched into four-wheel drive, got the revs just right, started in second initially, the wheels sliding a little at the back, but holding the line, staying in the tyre channels.

'Come on,' he said, his hands jiggling with the faux-leather wheel, keeping a loose grip, light and easy.

Feeling his way, the headlights revealing banked, crumpled shelves of snow, tiny flakes still wisping in the air. The vehicle shook in a blast of wind and the whole cabin moved, but he kept to the road, came up to the bend, turned around a black trunk which had broken down a low stone wall, and then he was on the last stretch, the steepest section, and revving again, maybe a little too much, you needed lots of revs for this bit but there was the smell of clutch and he had to be careful, the thing was moving left-right now, shuddering about, feeling all that power and noise as the wheels spun, he was going up fast, maintaining his speed, adjusting the wheel, all the time, pulling it down, left-right, spinning, slipping, he was nearly halfway up, she was holding the road, going up on ice, doing a grand job, ten seconds and he'd be there, at the topmost point, and then plain sailing from there home, or rather, not quite plain sailing but a lot easier and…

Who the hell was that?

11.

A figure, a woman, lit up in the road by the headlights, at her edges a strange, pulsing blackness…

He steered sharply to avoid her, the fine-handling of the vehicle lost in an instant, all his care thrown out the window, lurching sideways like a beast, a horse given its head, a helpless child on its back…

He felt the van swerve, his instincts reacting to correct it, then a greater swerve, the engine sounding like the vicious saw of a logging mill, his foot off the pedal, too late, *whomp*, into the side of the road, a moment of suspension – what's going to happen? – control is gone, what's beyond the road and… he's shaking and… will I die? And…

12.

He was sitting straight, in the dark, aware of the strange angle of the van.

There was no sound. The engine was quiet, stalled. But the lights were still on, their glare intensified by the white bank and tangled black vegetation into which they now shone.

He had come off the road. The van was up against the bank. Nothing appeared to be smashed, although damage to the front was likely. At least he hadn't slipped backwards, down the road. Who knows what would have happened then?

He wasn't hurt. Or at least, he didn't feel hurt. He couldn't rule out hidden injury, given the shock of the impact. The airbag hadn't inflated. Maybe the impact wasn't so hard. It was all a blur. And...

Where was the woman?

He twisted in his seat, looking upwards at the road. Dark. It was dark. Just the peripheral, fiery glow from his rear lights. But no sign of the woman.

'Shit!' he shouted. And again: 'Shit!'

His hands were shaking. He shifted in his seat, alert to the slightest movement of the van. Was she stable, or would she slide?

Things held.

He felt across, pulled the handle to open the door, thinking, please don't let there be door damage, that would be a very bad sign, but it opened easily enough, not getting caught in mud or blocked by a trunk. He stepped out carefully, down into a snowy trough, feeling tougher, knotted vegetation stop his foot from sinking too far. He moved away from the van, stepped back up on to the side of the road. The wind hurt, stung his cheeks. He looked at the Toyota, saw that, yes, it was tipped, just off the right angle, nose down, the front wheels possibly off the ground if it was suspended by the bumper, but he didn't think so. Didn't think it was grounded on the axle either, but couldn't be sure. The back wheel arches were high, but the tyres were still touching the verge – just.

'Hello?' He spun around, what was he doing, thinking about the van, when there was a woman in the road?

He looked, narrowing his eyes against the cold, feeling them go wet with tears.

13.

He went back to the cab, grabbed the torch, fumbled with the switch, then came back out on the road, swinging it around through the darkness.

Like the boy with the snowball, there was no one there. Just the cold, black, empty night. The wind had dropped, the snow was on the ground only, no longer filling the night air. Still, quiet. Nothing. He didn't shout again, just marched diagonally across the road, back and forth, shining the light into hedges, across broken walls, through the inky shadows of trees with their spindly, intrusive branches. Still, despite the weather, some crisp leaves were holding on in places, holding on by tiny threads.

Like the boy, that strange blackness limning her pale shape. Weird, like… like the strokes of a black marker, sketched by a child, held too hard to the paper. It wasn't the dark, that blackness, it wasn't something natural.

He felt a shrinking in his stomach, a deep, emasculating powerlessness. He didn't like this, didn't want to be here, he was stuffed, his only means of escape, of control against this dark, merciless night – his warm, safe vehicle – was gone, leaving him with… *this*. Something deeply wrong in the landscape. A woman, who wasn't a woman; a boy, who wasn't a boy. He rushed back into the cabin, slamming the door behind him. His eyes jittering left to right, but not turning his head as if… because he didn't want to look outside again. Didn't want to see anything. He could cope with being alone, out here, in the wasted emptiness.

It was *not* being alone he couldn't stand.

14.

He pushed the ignition, laughed when the engine started again.

He had a chance.

A chance to get out. All he needed was… for the wheels to grip, particularly at the back. One chance. A spin, and he was sure to be done for. But were the wheels firmly on the ground? The best thing, surely, was weight. Weight in the back. If only he hadn't already done the drop, not that the food was heavy, not in relation to a van. But it might have helped. Should he get out, pick a few of those heavy stones from the broken wall, drop them in the back?

He didn't glance sideways, didn't want to see that… woman, whatever she was, again.

Without thinking, he put the van in reverse and accelerated.

15.

There was the whirr of the spinning motor, the splatter of mud or snow, the cabin rocking, and then…

He was back on the road, moving fast, bouncing, jamming on the brakes to prevent another skid.

He stopped.

Somehow, he was now facing downhill. He realised he couldn't turn, there was no way of doing a one-eighty on this narrow lane, all he could do was go back down the hill. Back what, a few hundred meters, to the nearest passing place? And then come back, try to do this again?

No way. He hadn't made it this time, he wouldn't make it again. Especially if…

So what was he going to do?

He glanced in the rearview mirror, saw the orange-red of the rear lights on the piled snow like… like blood. He looked away, fearing what he might see. What was he going to do?

He needed to go back.

Back to the house with the woman.

The *real* woman. God, why did he have to think that, what were the implications of thinking that…?

16.

As he inched back down, on the brakes too much but thankfully scarcely slipping, he realised he had no choice anyway, the engine was damaged, the gearbox, he had trouble getting her into second, the clutch itself was wobbling.

When he came on to the level, he breathed a sigh of relief, but found he had to shove the gearstick forward three, four times before it moved into third. Fourth would be impossible, he reckoned. So he drove slowly, smelling the acrid, burnt rubber of the damaged clutch.

This was going to be expensive.

But that was the least of his problems. He needed to get to that house, to fall back on the Leslie family's goodwill. It was the season for it, after all, he thought, smirking at the bleak humour. He was going to have to call the breakdown as soon as he got reception, see if they would come out this far, on a night like this. They were going to be busy, lots of travellers, lots of last minute business, lots of accidents and stranded vehicles in remote places. He remembered the bad storm, Arwen, when all those villages were cut off, way back in '21.

But what other choice was there? It was hardly as if he could stay the night. How far was the nearest village? Probably five or six miles. Would they have a place to stay? A village pub with a room? What was the chance of that?

And he would have to walk. Through the dark snow, across country as there were no roads. With that woman, the boy anywhere…

No. He couldn't do that.

So what was he going to do? He should never have made this delivery. What an idiot! He remembered imagining earlier what Isla would have told him, imagined her telling him to get on with it, but now he realised she wouldn't have said that at all, she'd have asked him what on earth he was thinking of, was he nuts, risking a delivery in the dark in such treacherous conditions? God, why was he such a fool?

II.

Ashcraig

17.

Will, not would.

He needed to get his tenses right. Unforgivable. Isla *will* tell him he was a fool, next time they speak. He had to remain positive. But he was feeling it out here now, 6.45 on the clock, the smell of the burnt clutch disc filling the cab. He wasn't even sure he should be driving the van at all, what kind of damage might he be doing? He was no mechanic, but he knew he'd be needing a new clutch, at the very least. At least a grand, he reckoned. More cost he – *they* – could really do without…

The entrance to Ashcraig appeared, tall stone pillars topped with snow-capped, clawing griffons. The metal gates pinned back either side of the drive. He drove through, down the snaking avenue of trees, out at the end to the vista of the house. The high turret, pines, the open portcullis. Surely never used in defence, just a feature demanded by some Scottish Baron in the nineteenth century. Or Sassenach Baron, more like. Craving the symbols of status. *Sad.* He drove through the gate into the forecourt and, shaking his head, switched off the engine.

He sat there quietly, staring at the dashboard, the only sound the ticking of the engine.

'Jesus, Mary, and the bloody donkey,' he said, before clambering out and making his way toward the big oak door.

18.

He checked his phone for signal as he stood waiting.

Still nothing. He knocked again, then stepped back and looked up. The moon had emerged, a deeply gouged sliver of nail, with grey, mould-grey cloud to either side. Maybe that was it for the storm, he wondered. Hoped.

The same lights appeared to be on, a smattering upstairs and a few more down. He wondered if the girl might appear again. Then thought, was the whole family home? Mrs Leslie and the girl were all he'd seen, maybe the others were out somewhere? But then, the Range Rover was there – although of course they would likely have more than one car. The house was huge, easily big enough to lose people, big enough for them not to have heard him knocking. He didn't think there was anyone in the living room, as far as he'd seen or heard. Maybe Mr Leslie was sitting there in a red leather armchair, thinking his wife could do all the running around with the delivery man. He imagined an old, country gent, reading a paper in front of the fire with pipe and whisky. Pipe? Come on, you can do better than that… There was a tad – just a tad – of hysteria creeping in. His luck, the setting, the strange figures on the road. Harris, you're losing it, mate…

Still, the door hadn't opened. Was she a long way away? Maybe putting the babies to bed in some far quarter of the house, unable to hear him knocking. Oh, what the…

He would try one of the other doors. There was a large one on, what would it be, the eastern wing, to his right, near the base of the tower. A couple of smaller ones, one on the entrance wall, the other at the end of the car port on his left, possibly storage or work rooms, he guessed.

He approached the door on the eastern wing. It was quite a grand doorway, the substantial tower built out from the main, square footprint of the building. He saw through the windows a narrow, dimly lit gallery as he approached it. Then, looking in through the tall, latticed windows beside the door, he saw a large room lit by a blazing fire and solitary table lamp, as well as another Christmas tree – a library, with a staircase in the centre leading up to a second floor gallery in the tower.

It was a fabulous looking room. Despite being good at English at school he was no great reader himself, he didn't have the time, but it beckoned to him, that space. All those leather spines in the floor-to-ceiling shelves, the homely fireplace, cosy looking armchairs. He'd been better at science, studied Zoology at Edinburgh, but still, this place fired his imagination.

He checked himself. What if someone was watching him, peering in through the windows like some peeping Tom? He looked up and around again, but there was no sign of life. He reached up and knocked on the door.

At the same time, he heard a noise behind in the courtyard, the loud click of a latch. He turned and saw the main door opening. Rose Leslie stepped out in her long dress and called:

'You again? What are you doing?'

19.

'I'm so sorry,' he said, as he strode back to her.

'I had an accident…' An image of the woman edged in black flashed in his head. 'A bit of an accident, on the hill going back. Slid off the road and the engine's damaged. The gearbox. I had to come back down, as I wouldn't have made it and… my only option was to come back here. I'm sorry.'

She was watching him, a look of concern – or was it more akin to horror? – on her face. It was hard to tell, with her in the shadows. He felt himself blushing, his cheeks burning despite the atrocious cold.

'What do you want me to do?' she said.

'Is there any chance I could use your phone? I haven't got any reception at all.'

She looked at him. Her cheeks lifted, a semblance of a smile, then dropped again. 'Impossible, I'm afraid,' she said. 'The storm has knocked out the power, which has taken out the landline and Wi-Fi. It's happened before, back in Arwen. Luckily, we have a generator, keeping the rest of the house going. But the phones – no.'

'Shit,' he said quietly. 'I assume your line's digital?'

She nodded.

'The storm must have taken out some of the ISP infrastructure, then. Fibre nodes, cabinets…' He glanced down, frowning. What was he going to do? When he looked back at her, he was relieved to see her features had softened.

'Come in,' she said. 'Come in and we'll work out what to do.'

20.

'Would you like a hot drink? Or something stronger?'

She had led him into the living room, sat him down on the long sofa in front of the fire. It was covered in throws, very comfy, and the fire, its warmth, felt like a miracle after the ordeal he'd been through.

'I'd love one,' he said.

She was standing at the end of the sofa, her hand resting at the back of one hip. 'One or both?' she said. 'You look freezing. A cup of tea and a wee dram, to go with it? We have a nice Highland Park.'

He smiled at her. 'That would be *braw*, thank you, Mrs Leslie,' he said.

She looked at him, a little longer than he expected, then said: 'Call me Rose. And you are?'

'Ryan.'

21.

While she was out the room, he looked around. There was the gorgeous tree, twelve foot tall at least, draped in tinsel, wrapped in wispy cotton wool, giving a halo effect to its gleaming golden lights. There were cards on the hefty oak mantelpiece and strung beside it on decorative wires. Candles in silver holders stood along the mantelpiece, and there were two empty glass vases filled with fairy lights at either end. Beautifully wrapped presents had been piled around the base of the tree. Despite the size of the room, a good twenty-five foot long and twenty wide, it was warm. There were sheepskin rugs on the floorboards, woollen throws on the sofas, and plenty of soft, deep cushions. Cosy and warm. He began to relax.

But then the thought came again, what was he going to do? How would he get home? He couldn't think of any way of doing it. Unless someone was willing to drive him – but that was a very big ask.

What was the alternative? There really was none.

22.

He sipped the whisky, enjoying the fierceness at the back of his throat, the way the fire lit the ice with hues of honey and gold.

'That really is a very fine drink,' he said, taking another sip and sitting back with it in his lap. Rose sat down on the sofa, big enough that she was still a few feet away from him. She'd poured herself a glass of red wine.

'So what are we going to do with you?' she said. It sounded like an upper-class thing to say, but there was something mild and humble about her. Something humorous, ironic.

He shook his head. 'I really don't know,' he said. 'Perhaps, if they fix the power…?' He didn't think he could suggest her driving him. He thought about looking at the engine himself, but knew what a hopeless idea that was. You can't tinker with a gearbox.

'Yes,' she said. 'I guess that's the only option. There's Conlan village, I think there's a pub there with rooms – but that's five miles away, and you'd still have to go up the hill you had the problem with. Plus another challenge… I don't drive.'

He wondered if Mr Leslie was in. Could he drive?

'Are there any other houses down this road?' he asked. He knew it was a dead end, but thought there might be one or two farms or country homes like this further on. The road didn't stop at Ashcraig. 'Maybe a farmer who could help?'

'A good few miles, too,' she said. 'Not possible, really. They're likely to have the same power issues as us, we're all fed by the same infrastructure.'

He swigged more whisky, felt the pleasant warmth in his stomach. 'I probably shouldn't have come down here, after all,' he said.

'No,' she said. She gave him a warm smile. 'But thank you. It was good of you to try.'

As she gazed down at the fire, he couldn't help thinking, those green eyes, with their beautiful, starry flecks, they were really something... Stunning. Enchanting.

'It was the only chance we had to get our Christmas dinner,' she said, coming back to herself. 'Imagine, Christmas without the turkey and mince pies! And I'm sure we'd have run out of other things, milk and bread, too.'

Ryan turned his head, looking over his shoulder. He could hear faintly the radio in the kitchen still, the triumphant horns of that classical piece in Greg Lake's song, what was it called, Troika, that was it. He was expecting to see someone else.

'At least some good has come out of it, then,' he said with a chuckle.

'Where were – or are, hopefully – you going back to?' she asked.

'Newton,' he said.

'Will someone be getting worried?'

'No. But maybe later. Some people might be expecting me. Down the pub.'

'A few beers with the mates before Christmas?' she said, smiling.

He nodded.

'I'm sorry we kept you away from them,' she said.

'It's not your fault,' he said. 'It was all down to me to make the call on whether I could get down here. They won't mind.' He thought about the ice hockey, his eyes automatically searching for a TV but not finding one. Some posh folk kept their living rooms TV-free, didn't they? He imagined the kids in some snug nearby, watching Disney+, or more likely YouTube, given the age of the girl at the window.

Comfortable as it was here, he realised he needed to make more effort to get back and asked: 'Does Mr Leslie drive? Is he here?'

She looked quickly at him. 'No,' she said. 'He's not here. He's in Glasgow. He's not back until tomorrow.'

'Oh,' he said. 'So it's just you and the kids…'

'Kids?' she said. She turned and stared at him. Her face dropped, the loveliness vanishing from her eyes. He moved to stop her glass, as it seemed about to slip from her fingers.

'Yes,' he said, wondering what was wrong, had he said something…? 'The girl, your daughter… I assumed? I saw her earlier, upstairs, at the window?'

'Oh no,' she said, her voice catching in her throat. She stared ahead, at the blaze of the fire. 'No you didn't.'

'But… she was up there, looking out at me,' he said, feeling things swimming inside himself too now, like some power, a gravitational pull towards some hidden logic, leading him to…

'You can't have,' she said. Or rather, whispered.

'Why…?'

'Because I'm alone. There's no one else here but me.'

23.

He saw the look in her eyes, a deep, unsalvageable look of worry and despair. Realised something of that had been there from the moment he first saw her.

He was going to speak but stopped. They looked at each other as if time was like the weather, frozen. Horror was there, but something else, something that Ryan realised held promise, too. The only thing that could hold promise, with the creatures on the road, the girl in the window – understanding.

There was a connection between them, and sometimes connection was the last repository people had against a vast, careless, inexplicable universe. The true universe of nature, not the one neatly portioned up in our everyday stories.

He set his whisky on the side table, wiped his mouth. Looking at the fire, not her, he said: 'There are more. Out there, on the road. When I was coming down, first time, one – a boy, I think – threw something at the van, a snowball. It – the snowball – was real enough. I saw it melt on the window.

'Then, the reason I didn't make it up the hill, on the way back… she came out, of a sudden. She was there, surrounded by this… blackness. It made me swerve, hit the bank. I… I was so scared.'

'It's this place,' she said. 'I hate it here. It looks lovely, and we do so much to make it pleasant…' she cast her gaze around the room, at the tree, the fire, the drinks. 'But it's got a desperate spirit. It's reckless, haunted. Always has been, always will be. Always…'

He leaned across towards her, as she gazed into the flames. He'd never seen someone, a woman, look so desolate.

'Haunted how?' he said.

'I don't... how would I know? They just come. Particularly at Christmas. You'll find them anywhere, the house, grounds, the nearby countryside – the roads. Spirits. A woman, children, sometimes, most frighteningly – a man, so *angry*...'

Ryan couldn't help but glance around, to the dining room behind them, the door into the foyer, the one that was closed, at the far side of the room, which must lead to the library.

'It's hard to believe,' he said at last.

She looked at him wearily.

'I mean – ghosts? No one... I mean, they don't exist, do they...'

She closed her eyes, slowly. 'Tell them that,' she said quietly, her forehead creased.

'Where are they... sorry – do you have kids yourself?'

She nodded. 'They're with him. With Peter, in Glasgow. Harry, Georgina and Coran. They went down with him to visit the ice rink and do some Christmas shopping.'

'When are they back?'

'Tomorrow.'

So they really were alone together. 'Are they likely to realise that the phones are down? Do you think it might make them come back early?'

'I wouldn't expect so. I spoke to them this afternoon. When everything was still working.'

'Oh.'

Watching the side of her face in the firelight, he saw a tear slide down her cheek.

'Are you alright?' he said.

'You said it, didn't you? That you were scared. Well, I'm scared too. Petrified. I've always been scared. This place... it terrifies me.'

He moved closer, about to put his arms around her, then pulled back. What was he doing?

Nervously, she shoved the sleeve of her dress up and for a moment he noticed something, a scar, white, across the inside of her elbow. He frowned, and she saw him as she turned around. She pushed the sleeve back and looked at him.

'Ryan,' she said. 'Don't worry about trying to get back. Please – you can stay here tonight. I – I'd like you to. Please.'

24.

He leaned forward, elbows on knees, gazing at the hearth.

He took a deep breath and said: 'I will.' He felt her hand on his forearm and looked up at her.

'Thank you,' she said.

He opened his eyes wide and huffed. 'I'll be needing another one of these, though,' he said, holding up his empty glass.

'Sure,' she said, standing up. 'I'll get you one. But... are you hungry? Do you want something to eat?'

Now she mentioned it, he was hungry. Starving. Not only was it a long time since he'd eaten – a paltry prawn sandwich from the Coop in Newton, grabbed in between his morning drops – fear had a peculiar habit of making him ravenous. He remembered seeing The Exorcist with Isla and one of her mates when they were eighteen, how they'd devoured three large kebab and chips between them straight after, Isla's mate staring on in amazement as they just kept eating.

'I am,' he said.

'Are you happy with a sandwich?'

'I had one for lunch, but sure.'

'I could do something else, omelette or something?'

'Let me come with you,' he said. 'If you don't mind?

25.

He was a good cook, a grand cook, in fact, and after establishing what she needed for the family over the next three days he suggested he quickly knock up a spaghetti carbonara using some of the fresh pasta he'd brought.

'Are you happy to do that?' she said. 'I've got to admit, Peter didn't marry me for my culinary skills. He's the one who cooks…'

'Not a problem at all,' he said. 'In fact, it'll help take my mind off this – ,' he paused, holding back a swearword, '– day.'

She blinked assent, smiled. A brass band was playing God Rest Ye Merry Gentlemen on the radio.

'Do you mind if I leave you here a moment?' she said. 'I was running a bath when you arrived and need to let the water out.'

He looked at her momentarily, wondering how confident she was to be upstairs alone, after what they'd just discussed.

'Have it, if you want,' he said. 'If you're happy to… still go up there?'

'I might do,' she said. 'But… I might not close the door. I don't close any doors, in here, on my own so… don't come up.'

'I won't,' he said.

'Shall I leave this on?' she asked, looking at the radio.

'Why not?' he said. It was better than silence, that was for sure.

'Help yourself to wine, if you want.'

26.

There was no presenter on this radio station, so it was in one of the brief pauses between classical pieces that he heard the noise.

A single dull thump, from somewhere above.

He didn't think twice, dropped his chopping knife in the midst of the mushrooms and ran through the smaller door into the hall that connected with the foyer. A flight of balustraded stairs was at the end of the hall, turning at the halfway point to disappear from sight. There were tall, stained glass windows above the half landing, knights on horses, ladies in hennin headdresses, startled greyhounds, their colours dulled by the weak light of a small chandelier.

Ryan ran up, took the turn, ran up the next flight to the second floor where he found himself at the junction of a long corridor, leading to the southern, portcullis wall, and a wider gallery, in which he'd seen the girl. Nearby was a set of arched double doors, the left slightly ajar. The gallery had a runner carpet and paintings along the walls. The wall sconces nearby were alight, but further down both corridors vanished into darkness.

'Rose?' he shouted.

'Yes – I'm in here,' came a muffled reply, from beyond the door that was ajar. 'Don't come in…'

He moved close to the door, glimpsing a plush seating area with a fire above which hung a large portrait, and another open door set deeply into the wall beside the fireplace. He stared at the ground.

'I heard something – a thump,' he said loudly. 'Are you OK?'

'I am,' she called back. 'Don't worry.' A moment's silence. 'I knocked a stool over, that's all. When I was getting out of the bath.'

'OK, sorry,' he said. 'I'll get on with the cooking.'

'Thanks.'

27.

By the time she came back down it was half past eight, the pasta was bubbling and the cream sauce well underway in the pan.

He was supping a glass of red wine as she appeared in the doorway, in a different dress, dark red with a creamy, streaked pattern, spindly flowers. Despite the glow in her cheeks, her evident cleanness and limey soap scent, she looked troubled again.

'The food's nearly ready,' he said. 'Have some wine and sit down in the... where shall we eat it?'

'We can go in there, if you like,' she said hollowly, beckoning towards the dining room.

He gave her a pinched smile, then looked back down to tip in the small bowl of parmesan. As she walked out he thought, those marks on her arm, the scars, were they... could they be... self-inflicted?

28.

'You didn't see anything upstairs?' he asked, as he placed their plates on the candlelit table and sat down beside her.

She shook her head, picking up her fork.

'You look worried again,' he said. He tried his best, but as soon as he took a mouthful he could scarcely slow his eating, forking down the spaghetti. His stomach was growling with hunger.

'It's nothing,' she said. She twisted her fork in the pasta and lifted it to her mouth. 'Mm,' she said.

'You have a bit of cream…' said Ryan, pointing at the side of her mouth.

She wiped it away with the back of her hand. 'That's delicious. You *are* a good cook. Thank you.'

'I've always liked cooking,' he said.

'Is that why you set up this business?'

'Partly.'

'Tell me about it.'

'When I left college, I didn't want an office job. I wanted to do something that combined the things I was interested in.'

'Which were?'

'Animals – and animal welfare – I did a Zoology degree – good quality food – and the environment.'

'You wanted to save the planet?'

'Yes, to do my bit. So we – that's my sister, Isla, and me – we set up Fresh and Friendly, back in 2022.'

'So will she be worrying about you tonight, your sister? Will she know you're here? Oh – oh no, what is it? I'm sorry…'

He hadn't expected to cry, a grown man breaking into such a sob, his mouth full of spaghetti, in a castle in the middle of nowhere in front of a classy woman, how could he…?

She grabbed his wrist, leaned close to him. He managed to swallow the food without choking, pressed his mouth against the back of his other hand.

'I'm sorry,' he said. 'Please…'

There was a grinding sound, her chair scraping the floorboards as she stood and put her arm around his back. He squeezed his eyes tight, trying to stop the tears, but he could feel them dripping, literally, from his cheeks on to the white tablecloth. Could see them, making grey blobs.

'I'm sorry, Ryan,' she said, and pressed the side of her face into his hair. 'I didn't realise…'

'You couldn't,' he managed to say, between sobs.

She held on to him, his muscular shoulders and back, waiting for his crying to subside. Once it did, he felt her kiss the top of his head lightly, then she stepped back, sat down, and looked searchingly into his eyes.

'Would you like a moment alone?' she said. 'I can…'

'No,' he sniffed. 'I'll be alright.' He sniffed again.

She stood up, hurried into the kitchen and came back with a wad of kitchen roll. 'I'm afraid I haven't got any tissues,' she said, handing it to him.

He nodded, pulled off a couple of sheets and blew his nose. 'Thank you,' he said. He took a sip of water, then sniffed again.

'Aah,' he said, sitting upright, glancing at her. 'Hadn't expected that.'

'You've had a long and very bad day,' she said. 'Do you want to tell me about it? I'm happy to listen if you do, otherwise – whatever you feel's best…'

'Sure, thanks, no, I'm happy to…'

'What happened to her?'

He smiled, closed his eyes. At least he wasn't gulping down food anymore, he thought. He took a deep breath.

'She – she's alive,' he said. 'That's the most important thing, to start with. Isla is alive.'

He took a sip of wine, another deep breath.

'We were very close, you see,' he said, and sobbed again. Wiped his cheek. Rose was staring at him, concern in her eyes. She looked like she might be on the verge of tears, too.

'*Are*,' he said, grimacing. 'Are very close. Jeez – I keep using the past tense, it makes me so bloody angry…'

'So what happened?'

'It was May this year,' he said. 'She was coming home from a drop – we live together, in our parents' old house – on the A85. She… they don't know what it was, they suspect it might have been a stroke, a minor stroke or something, but she's only twenty-three. She went over the road. Hit an oncoming car. The driver, he was an old guy, a Falklands veteran. He was killed. Instantly, they say. They had to cut her out.'

'Ryan, I'm so sorry.'

'Yes, it took them nearly two hours. Paramedics on the scene, they had to treat her at the same time as the firemen – sorry, firefighters, there were two women there, they came to see me later – at the same time as they were doing it. Cutting her out.'

'My God…'

'They took her off in an air ambulance. To the Queen Elizabeth in Glasgow. Put her into a medically induced coma, operated for four hours but… she didn't regain consciousness.'

'She's still in a coma?'

He nodded.

'That's so hard for you…'

'It is.'

'Do you have other relatives – you said you live in your parents' house?'

'Yes, but they've both passed away. But yes, there are others – uncles and aunts, cousins, we all get along, but mostly they're scattered across the country, a couple in Aldershot, a cousin emigrated to New Zealand. The nearest is Uncle Miles, he's in Pitlochry. But we don't see him much.'

'It's a lot for you to bear on your own.'

'I have good friends, some still in Newton.'

'That's nice.'

His chest heaved, as he took one more deep breath. 'Look,' he said. 'That's enough about me and my sister. She's getting the best care she can. The doctors are a bit too neutral, but they haven't ruled out the possibility of a good outcome, they still say there's a reasonable chance. Let's change the subject, and try and enjoy the rest of this – very tasty, if I do say so myself – meal I've made.'

29.

'Do you work at all, Rose?'

They had talked a little about cooking, their favourite foods, he liked a good Aberdeen Angus steak and she was fond of seafood, squid and calamari, especially in risotto, but her absolute favourite thing to eat was honey-soaked baklava. Now they were back in the living room, with another glass of wine, sitting on the sofa.

'I do,' she said. 'I work in theatre – stage management, lighting. I've a small freelancing business, based in Aberdour.'

'What, across from Edinburgh? That's a way away.'

'Yes, it's where I started. Where I was living when I met Peter. We have a house now in the city. When I say "house," it's just a toehold really…'

'I can see your touch in the house, it's beautiful, especially the lighting. Despite what goes on here, this house – it's amazing.'

She smiled.

'What does your husband do?'

'Peter? You don't know?' She looked at him with her mouth open. 'Peter Leslie?'

'What?' he put his wine down on the table. 'The poet?'

She nodded.

'Oh – my – God.'

She shook her head. 'That's what they all say, when they realise.'

'Sorry,' he said. 'I mustn't…' He felt his cheeks flush, burning with the heat of the fire.

'Don't worry, I'm used to it,' she said. 'You're hardly the first…'

'I – we did him at school. What was it, Remote Season? It was a GCSE text…'

'Yes, that one.'

'I don't remember much, I've not got a great head for poetry. But there was one… something about love, falling into darkness like a lost god of the wood. I loved that.'

'Do you mind if I smoke?'

'Oh – sure.' He loathed smoking, but it was her house. Had he said something?

She opened an onyx box on the coffee table, pulled out a cigarette and lighter and lit up. Took a deep drag and blew a long grey cloud of smoke at the hearth. He had the feeling that something, their increasing camaraderie, was gone. Damaged.

'I'm sorry,' he said. 'Did I say something wrong?'

'No,' she said. 'Not at all.'

He was thinking, racking his brains for anything he knew about Peter Leslie. He was a renowned Scottish character, connected to the aristocracy, wasn't he an Earl or something? An academic, a lecturer in one of the universities. Famous for his poetry, although he wasn't prolific, just three or four collections, but all very well received. And that was all he knew – oh no, there was also his marriages, he'd had several wives, he'd only seen a picture of him as a young man, on the back of the poetry book, he must now be much older than Rose. And wasn't the rumour that he…?

'Sometimes I wish he wasn't famous, that's all.' She took another draw on her cigarette.

'It must be hard, I suppose,' he said, immediately unsure if that was the right thing to say. What did he know?

'It's not the fame itself. His work is beautiful, everyone knows that. Astounding. Amazing. It's the accoutrements of fame. They don't… lend themselves to family life.'

She wasn't looking at him at all as she spoke now. Instead, her eyes remained fixed on the blazing logs, which he'd replenished from a bronze bin when they'd come back after dinner. He decided to remain silent, wait for her to speak. Or not.

She smirked. 'Ryan,' she glanced at him, then said: 'This is a very odd situation we've found ourselves in. Two strangers, trapped by a snowstorm in a haunted castle in the Highlands. You could scarcely make it up. But – ' she twisted towards him, crossing her legs, 'I trust you. You're a good man, I can see that. And you've… you've had your fair share of suffering, I'm sorry to hear. But, I don't know, I feel I can… open up to you.'

He felt a stirring in his gut, something he didn't really want to feel. An attraction. She blew out more smoke, leaned back and stubbed out the cigarette even though she'd barely started it. 'My husband is very charming, very charismatic. But he is not a good man. Not a good husband – and not a good father.'

'Oh,' he said.

'I trust you're not going to be going to the Record with anything I say to you tonight?'

He shook his head, raised his shoulders a little, dropped them.

'That bastard has made my life a misery. There, I've said it.'

30.

'Jeez, it's a night for opening up, isn't it?'

Much to his relief, she laughed when he said it – it was something that could have gone so easily wrong.

'It is,' she said. It was her turn to take a deep breath. 'Look, you know what, there's ghouls out there, but let's fortify ourselves with more alcohol. Do you fancy a digestif? We have a gorgeous Port. Peter saves it for special occasions but, you know what? Sod him!'

Ryan laughed in surprise. 'Yes, I'll have one,' he said.

'Maybe if we drink enough, we won't even care if they show up again.'

She stood and walked off through the dining room towards the kitchen. As soon as she was gone, he realised he needed to pee. He hadn't been since arriving at the house, and they'd drunk a fair amount already.

'I'm just going to use your facilities,' he shouted.

'OK. Through the foyer, to the left of the stairs.'

31.

It was noticeably cooler in the foyer, he had taken off his woollen jumper in the living room but now, in his shirt sleeves, he realised how the clearing of the cloud was making this a truly bitter night. He worried about how he would be rescued, as the roads all around iced up. He could only hope there was no more snow. How likely was that?

But the worries only flitted through his head, a few minor blips within what he realised was an increasingly drunken, aroused state of mind. His thoughts weren't necessarily coming quicker, it's just they disappeared faster within the swirl of feeling. Things were good, he was excited, Rose was a real draw. Everything, he thought, glancing at a giant abstract painting above the door, blocks of mauves, browns, and lilacs across a field, was that meant to be a woman or a bird? – everything had switched this evening, it had started as the day from hell but was becoming increasingly special, enchanted even, he was really starting to enjoy himself, what would he be doing if he'd made it back home, nothing more than drinking at the Dogs listening to Rob bang on about Rangers' latest match, or Dylan's increasingly desperate attempts to find himself a woman…

And instead, he was here, in what was surely one of the finest dwellings in the land, drinking pedigree whisky and fine wine and sharing confidences with…

He stopped and shook his head in disbelief.

With one of the most beautiful women he'd ever laid eyes on.

32.

When he came out the bathroom, he shivered and noticed even in the dim light that his breath had misted.

Looking to his right, he saw a short corridor that led to a large door – which was ajar.

It must be the door to the car port, he realised. And if it wasn't divided into sections, then it must be letting in the cold air, as the set of doors near the entrance had been open – he'd seen the Range Rover in there. So he trotted down the corridor intending to shut it. But, as soon as he reached it, his curiosity got the better of him and he opened it fully to have a look into the giant garage.

Good grief, it was cold. Cold, dark and cavernous, with the only light coming from the distant, open double doors, at least fifty foot away, allowing in some moonlight. Nearby, he could sense as much as see another vehicle, possibly a worktop with tools. He could smell oiled metal and a dank, heavy wood odour, too. A workbench, for sure, he felt the metal arm of a vice as he reached out. At the far end, just before the Range Rover, there was some kind of partitioning shading the area to the rear of the vehicle, about the same height as it.

Was there a light switch?

He felt the wall to the left, the rough, cool stone. There – a set of switches. But when he flicked them, nothing happened. He fished his phone out of his pocket, interested to see what the other car was. He turned on the torch, swung the beam up. It was a sports car, a little vintage MGB, iris blue, with a soft top. It was jacked up, but in an odd position, as if someone had only just started to lift it. Tools were scattered around beneath it. Clearly someone's passion, he guessed Peter's, but then chided himself for making a sexist assumption. Maybe it was Rose, or perhaps one of the children, if they were old enough. He hadn't asked their ages, had he? He walked over to the Roadster, shone the light around inside. It was a neat little number, swish black leather seats, the speed dial in a wooden panel behind the steering wheel, the MG logo in the centre of the dashboard, above the ignition. As an environmentalist, he shouldn't indulge his love of cars; as nothing but a kid at heart, he couldn't help it. He'd love to give this little beauty a run.

He stood up straight, realising Rose would be wondering what had happened to him. He didn't want her thinking he'd been too long in the bathroom, didn't want her to imagine there might be something wrong with his stomach. God, was he developing a crush or something…?

Should he close the garage doors at the end? he wondered. In case they made a difference to the heat in the house? But as he looked towards them again, he froze.

Something had changed. He frowned, taking a moment to process what.

The partitioning by the Range Rover had vanished.

33.

He felt the blood in his thighs thicken, a squeezing, contraction, at his temples.

He lifted his torch, and pointed it over the top of the MG, down the length of the garage.

For sure, whatever it was that had been shading the narrow area between the vehicle and the back wall had disappeared. Had he imagined it?

He realised he wasn't breathing, his lungs had locked in his chest. He tried to suck in the cold air. He had to get back, back into the...

And then he saw it.

A pinpoint of pale light, flickering in front of the Range Rover, carrying its own halo of blackness.

Ryan felt a constriction in his chest, his stomach twist as he took in fast, shallow breaths. He wanted to turn, to not look, to flee into the warmth and safety of the house but still... something compelled him to remain there, to keep...

Looking.

As if we're compelled to bear witness, even when nature reveals itself to be bigger – far bigger, and far more distressing – than we ever realised.

The shape juddered. Again, he was reminded of a child with a black marker pen, frantically scribbling, creating a vivid edge to highlight... what? Just what was at its centre, its core?

There was no sound, but he imagined one, as if his ears had been soundly boxed as, in the next moment, the shape halved the distance between the car and him.

And now he could see, see more clearly, what that black enfolded. A face, a haggard face, scored with lines, the deep wrinkles of age…

But it was only generalised, an impression, he could not see the detail until…

34.

It vanished then reappeared right in front of him, a seething mass of hatred, burning anger, screaming into his face, dark eyes drilling into his, saliva exposed in that gaping mouth, grey teeth, black strokes shimmering all around like the striking snakes of a gorgon, a primal yell at the centre of that pasty, wrinkled flesh that went on seemingly forever until Ryan screamed himself and, dropping his phone, turned and fled back into the house…

35.

He slammed the double doors behind him as he came into the living room.

'What is it? Ryan? What is it?' Rose stood up from the sofa, scratching at her arm.

'Him!' he shouted. His eyes darted around the room, as if checking for more ghosts. The doors to the dining room were open, he lunged and slammed them shut.

'Who? The man?'

'Yes… God!' He was over at the fire now, backed up against it, staring hard at the door to the foyer as if any moment it would fly open, fall off its hinges.

Rose ran up to him, put her arms round his waist, watched too. In silence and dread.

36.

'I'm going to go and look.'

'No, don't,' he told her.

'We have to,' she said.

'It was terrifying. I've never seen anything… been so scared…'

'Who was it?'

'A man. An old man, with this kind of… blackness… all around him. In the car port. I went to take a look because the door was open, the cold was coming in…'

'I never left that door open,' she said.

He was becoming very aware of her arms around him, one of her hands on his stomach. He could smell the lime and cucumber scent of her hair, soft against his face.

'He was – he was *furious*. He moved so fast across the carport – one moment, he was at the far end, the next he was right there, in my face, screaming at me. Screaming, for God's sake!'

'Oh…'

He shook, held her tighter. 'It was… the worst.'

'We have to go and look.'

'No way.'

'I will. We can't – we can't just let him trap us in here… in my house!'

'Shit, Rose – he was… malevolent! Evil…'

She closed her eyes.

'What happened to him?' he said quietly.

'Who knows?'

They separated, Rose walking towards the foyer door, then halting, Ryan going up to her.

'We'll go together, if we're going,' he said.

37.

He let her turn the handles on the doors. He didn't want her to see how his hands were shaking.

Outside, the foyer was quiet, empty, the abstract painting of the woman in the field, the chandelier lit, but not so bright. There was a suit of armour – a suit of armour! – he hadn't noticed before, in one corner by the dining room doors, diagonally across from them.

'Over there,' he said, gesturing – as if she wouldn't know exactly where the car port door was. Idiot, he thought.

They walked – or, rather, took slow, tentative steps – across the giant rug spread on the dark floorboards.

'Calm down,' she said, reaching out and taking his hand. 'You're breathing too fast.'

He blinked, concentrated on expanding his belly, drawing breath down to the bottom of his spine. But it was hard, his mind filled with the ghastly, twisted mouth of that old man…

'You sound like you've seen him before?' he said, needing to talk to keep his panic at bay.

'Yes,' she said. She was pulling slightly ahead of him, leading him by his hand. Craning her neck as they approached the stairs, to see down the corridor to the garage door.

'Be careful, Rose,' he said.

'There's nothing there,' she said, as he came up to her shoulder. The door was still open, wide open, from when he'd run. Their breaths were misting with the cold.

'Let's have a look in the port,' she said.

He would rather not. He would rather run out from the house in a fit of madness, risk dying alone and cold in a freezing field than ever see that… *thing*… again.

But he followed her, down, into the long, dark, freezing space.

38.

'Uh – what's that?'

As soon as he stepped through the door into the garage, Ryan's foot half-slipped, half-stuck in something on the floor.

Rose, beside him, shone her phone at the ground.

'What is it?' she said, as they both bent down.

There was some kind of liquid pooled on the stone step.

'Agh,' said Ryan, as the smell hit him. 'That's disgusting.' There was a stench around the pool, a fetid mix of rancid breath and hydrogen sulphide. Rose covered her nose and mouth with her sleeve.

Ryan was about to put his finger in it but thought again. Instead, he glanced over his shoulder, saw the handle of a hammer on the workbench, and grabbed that. He pushed it into the viscous substance, which reminded him of a jellyfish he'd found as a kid, washed up on the beach in Scarborough. It stretched about, clear in places, milky in others, and seemed to cling to the shaft of the hammer for a moment before dropping back.

'It's like glue or something,' said Rose. 'But… that stink!'

They both stood up, Ryan directing his torch into the body of the garage, his anxiety returning with force after the temporary distraction. He swung the beam around, but it was weak and didn't show much more than the raised MG. But he could see there was no shadowy partition behind the Range Rover. What a relief.

There was a buzzing and long neon lights flickered into life over their heads.

'What – what did you do?' said Ryan, seeing Rose's hand on the light switches.

'Just turned on the lamps,' she said.

'When I tried them earlier, they didn't work.'

She shrugged, widened her eyes at him.

They made their way down the car port slowly, glancing about, checking apprehensively behind the crates, boxes and shelves that were concentrated in the middle section.

'We must clear this stuff sometime,' said Rose, distractedly. 'It's not as if we don't have enough storage elsewhere. Most of it's junk…'

As he approached the Range Rover where he'd first seen the old man, Ryan noticed again a strange odour.

Looking down, he saw a dark stain on the concrete floor. He knelt and at once had to cover his nose again.

'There's another patch here,' he said.

'It's not so thick,' said Rose.

'No,' said Ryan, standing up. 'If it wasn't for the stink, I'd have thought it was an oil stain.'

'Was this where you first saw him, you said?'

'Yes.'

'So the stuff…'

'Yes,' he said. 'It looks like it's got something to do with that creature…'

39.

Back in the living room, he added more logs to the fire and sat back on the sofa.

'Here – may as well drink these as they're poured,' said Rose, handing him the crystal snifter with the ruby port.

'Thanks.' He took a sip as she came and sat beside him with her own glass. His earlier spell of drunkenness had vanished but the port was still good, the aroma clearing his nose and reminding him of the Victorians, how they considered port a restorative.

'How long have you been seeing him – them?' he said. 'The ghosts?'

Rose sat back, rested her arm on the top of the sofa. 'Years,' she said. He noticed again the scar on the inside of her elbow before she unthinkingly covered it with her sleeve. 'So this place, it's been in Peter's family nearly two centuries. The first Lord Darnach didn't build it, but he bought it from the family who did only a few years after its completion, sometime in the mid eighteen hundreds. They had met financial ruin, something to do with fraudulent shares in the East Indian company, an early scam, and the head of the family fled in disgrace. He was never seen again by his wife and children, the rumours were he'd gone to Bolivia.

'Lord Darnach took advantage of the situation and bought them out at a fraction of what it was worth after taking over the loans which would otherwise have bankrupted them. I'm not sure there's much remembered about him, but I like to imagine him to be as much of a *c-word* as the current incumbent.'

Ryan shifted on the couch. His attraction to Rose didn't sit comfortably with her being married, but the way she talked about her husband made things both more complex and… possible. It was too much to get his head round, considering the blind panic he'd experienced a short while ago.

'Sorry,' she said, gazing at him abstractedly. 'It must make you awkward, hearing me say things like that. Peter being famous and all. I will rein myself in.'

'No, it's fine,' he said. 'I appreciate your trust in telling me. Your honesty.'

There he was, sprouting guileless gumph that set his cheeks on fire again. He looked down at his lap, but not before noticing a faint smile at the edge of those long, expressive lips.

'Go on, you were saying about the origins of them – the ghosts,' he said.

'Yes, I was. Let me come at it from another angle. I married Peter in – what, two thousand and fifteen. We spent much of our first six months together abroad, in Greece, where he loved to go to write. He had a small villa on the coast, just outside Kassiopi in Corfu. It was wonderful. He fished in a little boat as well, can you imagine? These poets, they have to live the lifestyle.

'But when we came back, we didn't go to Edinburgh as I'd have liked – he wanted to come here. I'm not much of a country person, so was apprehensive at first. But I grew to like it. Until one evening, I was sitting in the library reading and a bloody ghost appeared at the window.'

'Who was it?'

'A woman. Probably the one you saw earlier, on the road. When I told Peter about it, he admitted that the place was haunted.'

'Admitted? So he already knew, then. Had he seen them, too?'

'No… which was a cause of great frustration to him. He wanted to, very much.'

'Why? What a weird thing to wish for.'

'It was part of the old family tradition. Go and stay in Ashcraig and see the spooks. There's the Wicked Lady of the Black, the Boy of the Black, the Maid of the Black and – most terrifying of all – the Old Man of the Black. But – as you've found out – there's nothing funny about them, when you do see them. They are horrible things. Harrowing…'

She had been riding high on the story, but her face dropped as she said the last word. She looked desolate, wiped out – as she had when he'd first met her. He reached out and touched her arm, like she had with him. But she didn't smile.

She sighed and said: 'There was plenty of speculation about who the spirits might be. Some thought they were a family who had lodged here during the First World War, friends of the Baron, who had all caught the Spanish flu and died one after the other. But Peter didn't favour that theory, he thought it would have been remembered and passed down more clearly as a family favourite if it were the case. There was an idea that they might have been an older Highland family, crofters, killed during the clearances. That might explain the anger, particularly of the old man. Some thought it could be the original family who built it, the Hetheringtons, all distraught with tragedy, bitter and twisted by their fate.'

Ryan frowned. He was confused, bewildered. It was hard enough having to reframe his whole picture of reality to accept ghosts as real, but now, treating them as a mystery that could be rationalised, possibly even solved, was too much. How could you ever *solve* a ghost? Unless all that stuff those Victorian spiritualists and cheap TV psychics went on about, about helping them relieve their moment of crisis or injustice and pass over to the other side – unless that was somehow true? Jeez, what an idea…

'Of the Black…' he repeated. 'Is that because they're surrounded by that black pulsating stuff?'

'Yes,' said Rose. 'Peter told me his great-grandmother, something of a spiritualist herself – she wrote books about it – she said it was to do with the challenge for the ghost of coming through from the Other Side, from the dark space they inhabit. When I saw that woman at the library window, I told him how she was surrounded by it, like a mass of morphing coal, or liquorice. Glistening, black stuff. His great-grandmother, Connie May, she said it was because they had to force themselves through the membrane, using only the brute power of their hatred or anger. And she surmised, that explained the splash of liquid that came through with them sometimes. As if piercing the membrane to this world was like the breaking waters of a pregnant woman…'

Ryan wrinkled his nose. 'Shit…'

'It makes sense, doesn't it? Bizarre sense. The stuff we saw in the car port, of course. I hadn't been putting two and two together, but now… it makes sense.'

'But if that stuff comes through with them, isn't that, like, evidence? Evidence that ghosts exist? Surely people would be interested to see this? Ghost hunters? Scientists, sceptics, even?'

'I suppose they would be. But they come through so infrequently, and the liquid isn't always there. And when it is, it evaporates quickly. And it disappears, literally. Those patches in the garage – I suspect if we go back they'll be gone by now. The place where you first saw him, by the car – that was much thinner than the patch when he came up on you, wasn't it?'

Ryan thought about this, about going back to check. But realised, there was no way on earth he was going out there again. Not for a long time, not until his shredded nerves had a chance to repair.

'Does Peter have a view on who they are?' he asked.

'Yes. He reckons they're something altogether different. He thinks they are *bean nighe*, or similar creatures.'

'Bean nighe? What are they?'

'Superstition. The bean nighe would be the woman, maybe the teenage girl – because in local folklore they were always women – who washed the clothes of people about to die. Perhaps the man and boy were those who died?' She laughed, without mirth. 'Typical, isn't it? The women washing the men's clothes. Nothing changes.'

'Why did he believe something as weird as that?'

'You've read his poetry? All that stuff about myths, how they make us what we are? The First Story, or Stories, as he later came to define them. Well, he believed all that. Or at least made a good show of believing it.'

'And you?'

'I – well, I didn't but…' She closed her eyes and pressed her eyelids. 'There is something in it, perhaps.' When she looked at him again, there was something terrible there, a hollowness that made him want to put his arm around her there and then. But he didn't.

'Why do you say that?' he asked.

'The bean nighe is connected to another legend, or piece of Celtic folklore.'

'Which is?'

'Do you know the Irish banshee?'

'No. Or rather, yes, I've heard of a banshee...'

'She's the woman who keens. The one who wails at the approach of death. Not just wails, *screams,* in a way that daggers your heart. And... this woman, spirit, the ghoulish figure who haunts Ashcraig – how she screams!'

40.

For a moment, it was as if they had both been stunned into silence.

Then Ryan said: 'The old man – he was screaming at me...'

'I didn't hear.'

'Or it seemed so. Maybe...' He couldn't be sure. Had he just imagined it?

'When she screams, everyone will hear it.'

'You heard her?'

'Yes. That time in the library. One moment there was this face – haggard, but no so old – pressed up against the latticed panes – the next she was there, right in front of me, and I dropped my book and... she screamed. It was so horrible… right in my face, like she wanted to smash open the front of my skull, so she could then smash my brains… and my mind!'

He took hold of her then, and she buried her head in his neck. His eyes flitted across the tree, presents, cards, the accoutrements of Christmas, which now seemed so far away, a lifetime away.

What had he got himself into?

41.

'Did you ever see her again?' he asked, still holding her.

'No. But I saw the man and the boy once. Outside, down by the brook, one summer evening. There's a fording place, it can get quite deep with sustained bad weather – they were down there, standing straight, doing nothing. Just that black spew around them. I ran back here, twisted my ankle in my hurry. But the girl, no – I've never seen the girl.' She was gazing at the fire. His fear was tamed by the scent of her shampoo, replaced by a troubling desire. Troubling but appealing, as it seemed to offer the only distraction from the terror of this place. He was so attracted to her, he felt like he was losing control. Of everything.

'And what did Peter and your kids say? When you told them about the woman?'

'Peter is a child at heart. He was excited. He showed little or no empathy. But we didn't tell the children.'

'You didn't want to frighten them?'

'To be honest, I don't think they would have been worried. Georgina, Harry, even little Coran, they're very pragmatic, very much their father's children. Not mine. Well, they wouldn't be, would they?'

'Yes, I'd been thinking that,' he said. 'But I didn't want to say in case… Well, you look too young to be the mother of grown kids…'

'I'm older than I look,' she said. 'But yes, not *that* old. They're from his previous marriage. *One* of his previous marriages.'

He was out of his depth here. His own family was conventional, his dad a teacher, his mum a charity administrator, both happily married for twenty-seven years until cancer took first her, then him two years later. The only tragedy Ryan had known was his sister. If it wasn't for the pull of his attraction to Rose, desire keeping him focused, he would have lost it by now, for sure. Was he losing it anyway? He was just a simple bloke from a small town running a food business with his sister. And now look at him…

'The car,' he said.

'Huh?'

'How about if I drive your car? The Range Rover? I wouldn't want to try the hill again – but we could take it to one of your neighbours, further down the road, explain to them what's happened, ask them if they have phones that work – or at least a signal…'

She studied him for a moment. 'But what would we say to them? We've fled Ashcraig because of terrifying ghouls? They'd think we were nuts.'

'We – we wouldn't need to tell them that. Just say we need to contact the outside world – your husband, my friends. Get a message to them. We could work something out.' He was becoming excited. The idea of getting out was suddenly possible.

'What about the ford I just mentioned? If that's flooded and iced over, we might not get through.'

'It's not far, is it? From what you said. We can always turn round, or reverse. The Range Rover is good in these conditions. Snow, ice.'

He watched her face, thinking. 'Come on,' he said. 'It's our way out. We can't stay here like this. Something's got them going tonight, we need to get out – for our sanity.'

Her expression changed from consternation to a smile. 'You could be right,' she said. 'I don't know why I didn't think of it. Let's give it a go!'

'Brilliant!' he stood up.

'You're not too drunk to drive?'

'I'm over the limit, of course – but I'm fine. There's nothing like – whatever that *thing* was – to clear your head!'

She squeezed his shoulder. 'Great. Let me go and get the key.'

'I'll come with you.'

42.

He followed her through to the kitchen. The under-cabinet lighting was still on, and the radio too, playing something vaguely festive which Ryan recognised but couldn't name. It was oompah-brass band music, something that had been sampled in one of those 1980s Christmas hits.

He was wondering which one, when he noticed Rose had frozen ahead of him, staring down at a maroon ceramic bowl on one of the counters.

'What is it?' he asked.

He saw the worry lines on her face.

'The key,' she said. 'It's gone.'

He looked in the bowl. There were a number of keys in there, piled up – but none with a fob, none that looked like a car key.

'Are you sure it was in there?' he said.

'That's where they're always kept.' She touched the top of her head. 'Where else could they be…?' She looked around the kitchen surfaces.

'Who normally drives it?' he asked.

'Peter. We've got an Audi too, which he prefers. He took that yesterday. I wonder if he took the key by accident…'

'Is there a spare? There must be a spare somewhere.'

'There might be,' she said. 'But to be honest, because I don't drive… it's all Peter's responsibility.'

'Where might he put one? Think…' Ryan's mood was shifting from hope back to panic.

'Maybe… Maybe in one of his coat pockets or something?'

He followed her out into the hall, where she opened a small door beside the stairs into a cloakroom. He stood, nervously glancing towards the car port, as she rummaged through the pockets of Barbours, winter overcoats, lighter padded jackets.

'Nothing.'

'Does… might he have left them in the car?' They'd done it before, but the thought of going back in there still traumatized him.

'Not usually. But let's check.'

43.

'Shit!'

Ryan tugged the door handle futilely. The door of the Range Rover didn't budge.

'Shit, shit, shit…'

He had to stop himself from kicking the side of the car. Rose stood beside him, biting her thumb nail.

'Is there anywhere else it could be?'

Rose shrugged.

'What about the MG…' he began. 'No, that wouldn't do, it would never handle this weather,' he said, checking himself even as he had the thought. It was also clearly in the midst of work, so probably wouldn't even run.

'What are we going to do?' said Rose.

He looked at her.

'Drink,' he said, after a pause.

44.

They headed back into the living room via the kitchen, collecting the port and the whisky on the way.

Ryan stood by the hearth and lifted a couple of logs from the brass holder. 'What about some music?' he said, as he placed the first in the centre of the fire.

'What do you want?'

'Cheese,' he replied. 'Pure Christmas cheese.'

Rose smiled as she sat on the sofa, placing the bottles on the coffee table. 'Siri – play Christmas songs from… the last century!' she said.

A slow, quiet beat started up, like something creeping in from outside, feeling its way into the room.

'Band Aid – perfect,' said Ryan, tossing the second log into the corner of the fire. 'They should keep us going for a while.'

He returned to the sofa and sat down beside Rose, who was examining the bottles in the warmth of the firelight.

'Which first?' she said.

'Some more of your famous Highland Park, please,' he said, feeling a sudden abandon. Was he happy to be here, alone with her, after all? Despite everything?

'I didn't bring sir's ice,' she replied, with a small smile.

'No matter.'

They clinked glasses and sat back, propping their feet on the table and gazing at the fire.

Ryan spun his whisky in the glass, watching the molten gold make marvels with the firelight, then swigged.

'Beautiful,' he said. 'We drink enough of this and we won't mind if all the ghosts of hell rise up to visit us tonight. Especially with the two of us together. We can stay in here all night if we have to.'

He expected her to laugh, but she remained grave as she swallowed her dram in one. 'Too true,' she said.

'Let's try not to worry,' he said, looking at the side of her face. 'Come on.' He put an arm around her shoulder and, after a moment, she leaned into him.

'OK,' he said. 'Time to really take our minds off things. Favourite Christmas song?'

'Easy – I Believe in Father Christmas.'

'Greg Lake? Why him?'

'It's that line about the peal of Noel and the Christmas tree smell – it takes me straight back to my childhood, to one – or maybe two – particular Christmas Days. When I was eight or nine. We lived in this old Victorian flat, a conversion, it was the whole second and top floor of this big building on the corner of a fairly busy road. But it looked out over a beautiful park, with a gorgeous green hill sloping down to a lake. I loved that house. We had Christmas trees that I'm sure smelt more piney then. Maybe it was just the heightened senses of childhood. My mum used to spray the corners of the windows with that spray snow you don't see anymore, she used stencils to put snowmen and snowflakes and Christmas trees in the middle of the panes.'

'I remember that stuff. I'm sure some places still use it.'

'And the other reason I like Greg Lake is… like all the best Christmas songs, it deals with disillusion – and hope. He sees through the disguise.'

'I was never so sure about the end, about getting the Christmas you deserve,' said Ryan.

'A bit self-righteous, isn't it?' she said. 'Been assaulted? Change those clothes, love, they make you look like you wanted it. But I still love it. There's a germ of truth in karma.'

Ryan leaned forward. 'Whisky or port?'

'Umm…' Looking from one to the other, she raised her eyebrows for comic effect, like a child in a sweetshop. 'That one.' She pointed at the port. 'I like the pretty red colour,' she said, as he pulled out the cork and glugged a good measure into her glass.

'Shouldn't mix your drinks,' he said, handing it to her.

'Who knows where it might lead?' she said, taking a sip and raising an eyebrow at him. He blushed. She sat back. 'How about you?'

'Me what?'

'What's your favourite Christmas song?'

'Well it's not this one,' he said, as the rousing, star-filled chorus of Feed the World began to fade. 'I didn't like it much when I first heard it as a kid – then went completely off it in my thrash-metal teenage years – but I've come round to it now. I don't mind it at all, in fact.'

'Very noble of you,' she said with a grin.

'Yes, it's the patronising bits – which I guess is part and parcel of most Christmas songs. But I get the historical context now, the goodwill that was meant. Sir Bob's moral drive, and all that.'

'And so…?'

'Let me think…'

From the speakers, a new singer began humming with the warm opening cords of the next song. 'Well – I do like this one,' he said.

'Johnny Mathis?' She knocked his arm with her glass and a little port splashed over the rim on to his sleeve. He didn't care. 'You just mentioned cheese…'

'I love cheese,' he said. 'Christmas is all about cheese. Like you say, the songs you love the most are the ones that bring back the most. That initial, starry-eyed feeling about Christmas. The excitement, carols, the little family rituals.' He thought about Isla, knees apart on the floor, with pigtails and her reindeer jumper. Chattering a set of toy teeth in front of her mouth, mimicking the voice of Mr Bean, making the whole family crease with laughter. She was a delight, still was. *Is.*

'But then there's something else, something that makes it magical, instead of just fun,' he continued. 'It's the – now you're going to laugh at me – it's the sacred quality. The sense it's underpinned by something bigger than just presents and the warmth of a mother's love…'

'You're not going to get all religious on me now?' she said, elbowing him.

'There you go – mocking me, like I said…'

'So do you believe? In God? Jesus? Christmas?'

'I have a kind of faith,' he said. 'But I don't go to church or anything.'

'What do you believe?'

'That there's something. Something bigger than us. God – I suppose God can be just a word for everything – but yes. Ha!' he blushed, laughing at himself now. 'I guess I believe in something spiritual, that's probably the only way to describe it. There's something we connect with, when we have that feeling of holiness. Sacredness. Something real, not something delusional in our heads.'

'Sounds like you're a closet Christian to me.'

He laughed. 'Perhaps. But I don't believe in an old man with a white beard in the sky.'

'No Santa coming down the chimney for you, then?' she said.

They laughed again, then both were quiet for a moment, his words making him suddenly think of the Old Man from the Black.

'How about you? Do you believe in anything?' he asked, to dispel the uncomfortable silence. He wanted to get back to the fun they'd been having, the distraction.

'No. I think it's all make-believe. A load of old baloney. Like Christmas itself.'

45.

'That's cheery.'

'You can tell I'm scarred.'

He thought about the wounds he'd seen on her arms.

'Are you?' he said, turning to look at her.

She grimaced, her lips crinkling. 'I guess,' she said, with a shrug. 'You can't spend the best part of five years married to a narcissist without something giving.'

'Is it really... is he that bad?' he asked. He was doing his best to sound caring because... because he did care. Really.

'He isn't... well, I suppose you couldn't call him an evil man. Not violent. Or at least physically. He pours all his brutality – of which he has a fair amount – into his poems.'

'I remember, that one about the lion, eating a bird, a vulture. Swatting it down, repeatedly, just playing the Lord of Destruction. That was a powerful poem. For me, as a kid.'

'Yes, that one always goes down well with the punters. And the one about the shark, the Great White, as an ambusher. *You in your dark, directly below...* He's never hurt me, though. Never hit or smacked his children. No, he saves all his violence for his art. And for the casual emotional flaying of those closest to him.'

'Emotional flaying?'

'Humiliating putdowns, often disguised as jokes. Very funny. And neglect. He's never here, never with you. Always promising, never turning up. And – you know, I've told you now – the affairs. Which was half of why he doesn't turn up. And the other half – no, quarter – is because he finds something better to do. Gets a better offer at the last minute.'

'And the other quarter?'

'That's his perverse side. He sometimes does it purely to wound. To keep you wondering what he's up to. He knows hearts and minds, you see. Knows how to play with them. How to mess them up.'

'He sounds more like a psychopath than a narcissist.'

'Perhaps he is.'

'Have you thought about leaving?' He wanted to mention the scars on her arms, had she ever self-harmed? Or worse, tried to kill herself? Because of this monstrous ego, this twisted excuse for a husband. But he couldn't mention it, he knew.

'Leaving him?' She swigged her port. 'Yes. Many times. Just last night, in fact. He didn't invite me to Glasgow with the children. He could have but didn't. He knows I don't like it here on my own. Just more of his mind fuckery. Yes, I think about it all the time.'

'And...?' A wild image flashed in his head, of marrying her. Standing at an altar in some remote country church, her dressed in white, her dark hair hidden beneath a veil, red lipstick, her green eyes shining bright at him as she took the vows... He shook slightly. Where did that come from?

'Are you OK?'

'Yes, yes, fine,' he said.

She took another cigarette from the onyx box, lit up. 'I suppose I will... one day.'

He was still struggling to regain his train of thought after that crazy image. He was worried he might say something stupid, uncontrolled, drunk, something he didn't mean to say. So instead he squeezed her arm lightly.

She blew a cloud of smoke at the roaring hearth. Some crooner was delivering a version of Silent Night on the sound system. Ryan felt his head do a little twirl, not quite a full spin. He was getting drunk now, all this stress and unfamiliarity…

But at the same time, he was comfortable. He drained his glass and poured himself another whisky, then sat back. Naturally, his arm went around her shoulder again, and they slid down, glasses in hand, Rose flicking her cigarette into a shallow ashtray she'd placed on a cushion. They went silent for a while, listening to the soft music.

Pressed up against this beautiful woman, Ryan's mind began to drift. The old man, the woman in the road, girl at the window, the snowballing boy… all reared up but were swept away by an increasingly strong sense of peace, security, caused by the attractiveness of the hearth, the lulling songs, the sweep of intoxicated blood through his veins, the warmth of the woman beside him, pressed against his side, smelling sweet and soft, like – like he was home…

…*slee-eep in heavenly peace*…

46.

'Isla…'

'Huh?'

He opened his eyes, felt Rose shuffle against him. Looking down the side of her face, he saw her eyes half open, gazing at the fire.

He had fallen asleep. Woken up with an image of… what? Of his sister, with her short brown bob, in her hospital bed, wired up to life supporting apparatus. But she didn't have a bob now, it had grown out. Had she… had she opened her eyes?

In his dream?

'What was it?' said Rose. It looked like she'd been sleeping too. The music was still playing, a song he didn't recognise, but it sounded like Kate Bush.

'Nothing,' he said. 'I fell asleep.'

'Did you say something about your sister? Isla?'

'I must have been dreaming about her. I think…'

Somehow, Rose's arms were both around him now. She must have cuddled up whilst they were both asleep. She squeezed his waist.

'Poor baby,' she said.

It was an odd thing to say, he thought. She looked up at him. It was so natural then to kiss her, he just had to lean his face down slightly and their lips met.

The loveliness of the room, the candlelight, music, Christmas tree, fire, all was subsumed into his awareness of her. Things changed as they kissed each other's mouths, harder and deeper. He felt himself becoming something else, reaching with his hands, feeling her dress, her flesh, pressing with his hips, time changing rapidly, changing, time itself changing. Time ceasing to happen, he was no longer processing things in the same way, he was aware of the room, the space around him, but also not aware of it. He was consumed by sensation, by love, by something else, by the crux of what he really was – hope, or at least desire. Intense desire.

When, what felt like no time later, they'd finished, it was hardly what counted.

What counted was how he had reached the highest part of his mind, higher than ever over the earth, the earth gone, and been left with nothing but blinding light, the only place he'd ever wanted to be – the place of arrival.

47.

It was only afterwards, as they lay there, shaking with breath, that he realised how awkward they had left themselves on the sofa. Bones against bones, limbs pinned against limbs.

Rose seemed to realise at the same time as him, and they shifted themselves around, pulled their clothes back so they were once again upright, fully aware, and... awkward.

'I... I never expected that...' he said, feeling he ought to speak. 'Rose, if you...'

'Shh,' she said. He was concerned by the troubled look on her face. But it was momentary, gone in an instant. She looked around at him and smiled. 'Let's have another drink,' she said.

It seemed the right thing to do. He poured them both large whiskys and they sat back, a little more rigidly than before. Shit, he thought, I've blown it, I've just had sex with a married woman, a customer... He looked at her again, his face forming a weak smile, which she returned, equally feebly. She lit herself another cigarette, for something to do to distract from the thing that had come between them, the intensity, he thought. What was she thinking? Probably that she'd made a terrible, terrible mistake. It was one thing speaking about the antics of your lowlife husband, quite another to shatter the bonds of marriage yourself. Did she hate him too, now?

The Christmas songs had kept going of course, and in the interlude between Silver Bells and the next he heard a whirring sound, initially alarming before he realised it was the wind pressing the windows into their frames.

'It's picking up again,' she said. And then, deliberately, as if to reassure him, she leaned back into his side and once again his arm was around her shoulder. He felt a flood of relief, a genuine flood, as if his blood was again warm and flowing. He relaxed against her.

'Do you think we ought to try anything else?' he said, nuzzling her hair. 'To get out, I mean!' he added, as she burst into laughter.

'I was getting quite excited for a moment,' she said, still chuckling. 'What else could we do?'

'Search more for the keys to the Range Rover? Maybe try the MG? What is there to lose?'

'That's hopeless,' she said. 'We've looked everywhere I can think of. And the MG, it hasn't been in a drivable state for years. Peter's always tinkering with it, ordering specialist parts on the internet, through friends of friends. It's really not worth it.'

He reached around, moving his hips awkwardly to try and ease his phone out of his pocket. Still no signal. 'How about the power? Should we check in case the line is back?'

48.

They checked the phone in the foyer.

Outside the front door Ryan could hear the wind, hear it pressing the windows on either side, despite the secondary glazing.

The phone when Rose picked it up was still dead, the same with the internet router, which showed no lights.

'It must have damaged the main power line,' he said. 'Otherwise I guess the generator would have reconnected you.' But he didn't really know much about power supplies. He peered outside, could see the van in the pale light from the house. Tiny flakes of snow were being whisked about in the wind. He shivered, thinking of the cold.

49.

They sat back together in the warmth of the living room.

'Final nightcap?' said Rose, holding up the port.

He nodded and smiled. 'Guess that's it, then,' he said. 'We're here for the night.'

'Suppose so,' she replied. 'But we'll be safe. The ghosts – they only ever seem to come when you're alone.'

'That's a relief,' he said. 'We're safe together.' He wished he could believe it. Another song started up, folky, with an upbeat male vocal.

'Now – this one I love,' he said.

'What is it?'

'Gordon Lightfoot. Song for a Winter's Night.'

'Never heard of it.'

'My dad used to play it all the time,' he said. 'He was a child of the seventies. Loved his folk music, Archie Fisher, Silly Wizard, Joni Mitchell…'

'Silly Wizard?' Rose snorted.

'Yes, they were a Scottish band, very popular back in the day…'

They chuckled, listening to the gentle song, the starting of the Christmas bells.

'Song for a Winter's Night,' she said. 'It's nice. Yes, I like this one.'

'When I was growing up I was embarrassed by it,' he said. 'Embarrassed by him, my dad, I guess. With his woolly socks and angling, his singing in the church choir. Every Sunday, a hike up Ben Loran, our nearest hill.'

He paused, then said: 'But I love it now.'

'We change,' she said. 'We really do change…'

III.

The Night

50.

When he woke up, he was surprised to see two children sitting at the base of the tree.

The boy, in front of the fire, was the youngest, probably about twelve years old. He was wearing a bobble hat, odd considering the heat, and facing away from him. The girl was in her middle teenage years, proud, back upright, reaching down for one of the presents and looking at the boy with a big grin on her face. She had long, auburn hair and pale, Scottish skin, and was wearing a dress that at first seemed Victorian to him, but when he looked longer he realised it was more modern, just a nice, white cotton dress like any girl from Newton might wear out for the night, or to the shops.

The boy was saying something, something about Atari, was it?, he was looking forward to playing a new game, a computer game. The girl hoped she got the watch she wanted, a new Apple watch with all the fitness bits and bobs. The apps.

Rose was sitting beside him, watching the children too. She looked at him and her broad mouth broke into a smile.

'Our children,' she said.

Without replying, he looked to his right because there was the noise of the door being opened.

A man and a woman stood there, both old, so old, with wrinkling skin and stooped backs, but both dressed smartly. He was wearing a neat, blue lounge suit, double breasted, with a handkerchief folded in the pocket. She had a long black lacy dress. He realised that she was other than he'd thought, his first impression was that she was young, or middle aged, normal looking, with her hair tied behind her head, but now he saw that she was someone else altogether, in fact her face was entirely covered by a black veil, like a mourner.

'What do you think, Mr Harris?' said the boy, looking around over his shoulder. 'Should we open the presents before or after Mr Lightfoot?'

He felt the weight of indecision. An obstacle he couldn't get around. Should they open them before or after Christmas pudding? They could do with a break, their stomachs were full. Bursting.

He was going to ask Rose, she would know what to do. But then there was the noise of a howling wind outside the stained glass windows. He turned to look round and stopped – although of course, he wasn't moving, he was just sitting on the couch – he stopped, or rather, things stopped, the people in the room, even the flames in the fire, as he noticed, standing in the corner, a normal person, a normal woman, but in the shade, away from the fire, away from the candles, away even from the muted glow of the tree –

In navy boot-cut jeans, in a Glastonbury T-shirt, with short, bobbed hair –

His sister, Isla.

51.

He woke with a sharp sniff.

Blinked, and rubbed his eyes.

His mouth was dry, had the rawness, the fume of alcohol about it.

The fire had burned down, but a soft flame wrapped repetitively around the remains of the great log he'd placed in the centre. The tree was glowing. Shakin'

Stevens was singing quietly about a blue Christmas. The bottles stood, purple and gold, mostly drained of their contents, between him and the fire. But something had changed. He knew it, he…

Rose.

Rose was gone.

52.

He looked around the room.

Stood up, checked behind him, the area behind the sofa, the shaded, recessed section at the far end of the room near the window, the place where…

Where Isla had been standing.

Isla?

What…?

He raked his fingers through his hair. In his dream. He had been dreaming. In the dream, Isla, his sister, had been standing over there, in the corner, silently watching…

Silently watching what?

He turned, checking the doors. They were both closed, the double doors to the dining room, the single door to the foyer, the door to the gallery and library beyond. They had closed them all to keep in the warmth, as the night grew colder. What time was it? There was a clock on the mantelpiece, an old, ornate carriage clock, wrought gold – or gold plated, certainly – with a red surround.

2.15! What had happened to the time? How long had he been asleep?

Had she gone to the toilet? Maybe she'd just woken up, desperate to wee, not surprising after the amount they'd drunk, got up and gone out without waking him…

Isla.

He'd dreamed of Isla, standing in the corner. With a boy and a girl, a teenage girl, by the tree. By the fire. Opening presents. In his dream.

The boy had talked about an Atari. That was old. But then the girl had talked about an Apple watch, and that was new.

Dreaming. Just the mess of a dream. He had a headache.

What was he going to do?

Move out, find Rose.

Move out into the house?

Fear clutched him, made him wide awake. The image of the Old Man of the Black, screaming into his face, his mouth, those yellow teeth. Never felt so much terror…

They only come when you're alone…

Oh shit.

What was he going to do?

He sat back down on the sofa. Shakin' Stevens continued to croon about how bad his Christmas was going to be without you. Ryan leaned forward and put his head in his hands, in alarm.

Wait.

He should wait. Give her a minute. He remembered how he was like, with his last girlfriend, Bella, when they slept together. She would always get up in the middle of the night to go to the loo and it would wake him, but never at once. He always woke a minute or two after she'd gone, normally just before she was coming back into the room. And she didn't flush, not in the night, so it wasn't because of the noise. It just took him a while to wake, when he was disturbed by something.

So perhaps that's what had happened here.

Rose had got up and left him to go to the loo, and it had taken him a while to rouse properly. Maybe that was when he'd started the dream. The dream about the teenage girl, the boy with the bobble hat, Isla... And the man and the woman!

There was a man and a woman at the door, wasn't there? Except the layout was different, it was a different door, and there was only one, in the middle of that wall, in between where the real doors were, the one to the foyer and the other – the double doors – to the dining room. They'd come in through a different door. They were old, one was smart, the man, the other was middle-aged, an elegant woman… who had shifted, in the dream, transformed into a woman in black, a long veil, a threatening presence, there was doom around her, he felt it now, although in the dream it had been less so…

Rose!

Where was Rose?

He needed to do something. What was he going to do if she didn't come back?

53.

The other possibility was that she'd woken up hungry – or thirsty. Parched, because of all the booze. Gone to get some water.

He should check the kitchen.

He could feel his heart, it was beating at a good pace, perhaps one-and-a-half times normal, maybe one-ten per minute. He was…

'Siri – shut down!'

Shakin' Stevens was stressing him out, he needed to think.

But the silence, when he was gone, was deep. Oppressive.

Just the faint rustle of the fire now. Nothing else. Not even the wind at the windows, as it had been when he fell asleep for the second time. No more whistling.

Ryan took a deep breath. Felt his heart pulse, firm, steady, upbeat as he held the air in his chest. Let it out slowly.

He was OK. He… he would keep those thoughts of the ghost – *ghosts*! – out of his head.

He would go check the kitchen.

54.

She wasn't there.

The quiet, classical radio station was still playing. No longer Christmas music, something quieter, on the piano, Rachmaninov, he thought. The room was still lit softly by the under-counter lights. The maroon bowl was full of keys, key rings with fluffy balls, key rings with leather tags, key rings with nothing but keys. The pan he'd used for the carbonara was still on the hot plate, caked in sauce that had darkened to brown. His plate, her plate, stacked together on the counter above what he guessed was the dishwasher unit. She had brought them out, she would have put them over the dishwasher.

That's what people did. There was a can, a can of black kidney beans by the plates. Something he'd not put away earlier. The bean nighe, he thought. *Bean nighe…*

Should he shout her name? It might be the quickest way of finding her. But…

Shouting would let *them* know.

Let the ghosts know he was here. On his own. Scared.

Absurd. Irrational. Could ghosts even hear? What a ridiculous thing to be thinking about, could ghosts hear! He was a twenty-four-year-old man, fit as a fiddle, almost two hundred pounds of muscle thanks to the workouts he did, the ice hockey and footie he played, down the rec, the five-a-side with his mates, Rob, Dylan, Sticky, Dave, he wondered if they missed him down the pub, down the Two Dogs, downing pints of Gunn, one after the other…

Compose yourself.

Compose yourself, man.

God, he was sounding like them, like one of the English Overlords. What? What a stupid thing to think, it wasn't the bloody nineteenth century!

Just… get a grip, Harris.

55.

He went out into the hall, by the stairs and toilet. Saw the cloakroom, the passageway to the car port, where the door was shut. He remembered. Remembered the slime on the floor.

Turned to the toilet door, put his face close.

'Rose? Rose – are you in there, love?' Love? He called her *love*? Was he nuts?

He reached up, tried the handle. There was a click, the door swung inward.

On an empty room, of course. Although there was a whispering sound, what… He tugged the light switch cord, the overhead lamp came on.

The tap. Hot tap. It had been left on slightly. There was steam coming from the thin line of water that leaked into the stained plug hole. He switched it off.

Had he left the tap on? He couldn't remember. How would you remember something like that? He'd used it, of course, washed his hands with the orangey-smelling Molten Brown handwash.

He couldn't remember.

Perhaps she'd come out, washed her hands and then… gone upstairs? Had she gone to bed? Maybe she'd woken up, beside him on the couch, aching from their slouched positions, come out, gone to the loo and washed her hands, felt drunk and miserable, could no longer care less about the stupid ghosts, just wanted her nice, comfortable bed. Went upstairs on her own, no need to wake him and tell him, why should she…?

That felt likely to him. What were the alternatives? The car port? He looked down there, looked at the floor, it was clear, the slime, ectoplasm, whatever it was, was on the steps on the other side of the closed door…

Why would she go out there? To check for keys again?

No. He wasn't checking the garage. Not on his own, not now.

Perhaps she was on the other side of the house? Gone through the living room into the gallery he'd seen when he was outside, down to the library?

Why? Why would she go there? No one wanted to read after a couple of hours' slumber, after a shedload of booze. Besides, if she was a reader, her book would be somewhere else, not in the library, by her bed or something. She wouldn't go to the library to read in the middle of the night, not when there were ghosts in the house.

He looked at the staircase, up at the knights and horses and dogs and ladies on the shadowy windows.

Upstairs.

He would go upstairs.

He'd been before, it was alright. He would go again. See if she was in bed.

56.

Christmas Eve.

It was Christmas Eve, he realised, as he climbed the stairs.

He couldn't imagine ever feeling less in the festive spirit than he did now. *Ever.*

Halfway up the second flight of steps he stopped, gripping the banister. He listened.

There was a feeble moan, the wind against the windows or the eaves. There was a click, or rather tick, probably the heat in the radiator pipes, but arrhythmic, so possibly old wooden floors, doors, the framework of the house settling, contracting in the cold. And… there was another tick, faint, this one persistent, surely some sort of clock. He looked back down to the half landing, the tall windows above it. Noticed the fleur-de-lys decorative work around one of the middle panes, the pale, unworn face of a young man, his soft lips and thick brown hair. Probably some noble's son, wearing a blue tunic, looking at a sheep below in a field. Or more likely gazing at the rose-lipped woman beside it, in her conical hennin. A lover, then, fresh to love, undamaged by the world, with a surplus of energy he's about to squander on romance. How would it end?

Ryan thought about the spirits. Standing there, in the relative quiet of the stairs, he remembered when he'd first watched *Jaws*, aged nine or ten, at a friend's house on a Saturday afternoon, the parents out. It was thrilling, frightening, cushioned in the safety of Laurence's den. Then, the summer after, on a family holiday on the Costa Brava, his dad had taken him snorkelling, away from the kids splashing at the shore, out into deeper water. He had been looking around, from the surface, perhaps twenty foot down to the murky, brown stones on the seabed. And an image of the film, the woman at the start, being seized at dusk, from below, came into his head. He'd begun spinning, spinning around on the surface of the sea, looking behind him, around him, down, along the bouncing, silvery level where the water changed to air, panicking because he thought there might be a fin there – or there – or there…

Until his dad had come over, pulled his shoulder and, after making him lift his head and breath properly out of the water, reassuring him that there were no sharks here, no sharks in the Mediterranean at all – something he found out years later was a lie, not a small lie but a huge whopping one, Great Whites *bred* in there – had swam back with him to shore…

After that, he'd never watched a shark film again and, whilst it didn't stop him going in the sea, whenever he did he had been aware, especially when out of his depth, of the darkness below, and the full-scale terror of what inhabited it. Because the sea had no walls, nothing to separate him from any monster of the deep.

He thought about the rooms behind him, downstairs, the living room, kitchen, dining room, library, carport. He thought about the rooms above him, the bedroom with its hearth and bathroom, many other bedrooms, he assumed. And he thought about *them*.

They were in here somewhere. Or were not. He had to hold both possibilities in his head at once. Like the sharks – almost certainly not below him, he knew, the probability vanishingly small, but still real – they could be about to spring on him any moment, to break through whatever black membrane separated their world from this, and scare him witless.

Scare him to death.

That was the phrase, wasn't it? Scared to death.

What if the man came at him with his horrific scream, so sudden it literally stopped his heart? He had locked his breath in his chest, so why not that pumping lump of muscle too, next time? With Rose gone, there was no one to save him, no chance of a call to the emergency services anyway, with the line dead.

God, he was talking himself crazy.

With a glance back over his shoulder at nothing, he continued up the stairs.

He had to find Rose.

57.

At the top he stopped, looking down the landing to his right that led towards the southern wall with the portcullis, then at the broader gallery ahead, where Rose's room was – and where he'd spotted the girl at the window when he first arrived at this cursed place.

He wondered if there might be some of that stuff, the ectoplasm or whatever, where she had been standing. His stomach turned.

The hall to his right was gloomy. The nearest two or three sconces, glass lamps styled like flames at head height, were on, but not those further down – so the corridor disappeared into darkness. From the orderly spacing of the three doors he could see, he guessed these were bedrooms. Probably for guests, or maybe the kids' rooms. Georgina and Harry, wasn't it? And Chris – no, something less usual than that, *Coran*, that was it.

Most importantly, there were no shapes emerging from the darkness at the end of that corridor.

He turned, took a few steps forward and looked through the first tall, latticed window of the gallery. The Toyota was still there, his wounded steed, now covered in a thin layer of snow. Wounded steed? The castle was starting to get to him, making him think strangely. It could scarcely be called a castle anyway, just a piece of Victorian mock-gothic architecture. Delusions of grandeur amid the nobility, or would-be nobility.

He walked up to the double doors of Rose's bedroom. The lefthand door was ajar, like before.

Through the gap, he could see the fire, almost burned down now, just a few fireflies dancing around a blackened log, the hint of orange in the white ash. He assumed this was the seating area for the bedroom, which was almost certainly in darkness except for the firelight. It would have been a romantic and cosy spectacle with the portrait and the armchair but... not now.

Ryan thought. Should he go in? What if she was in bed? Was it an invasion of privacy?

They'd had sex, for God's sake...

He pushed the door inwards, hearing the faint creak of the hinges.

And walked into the room.

58.

As he'd guessed, there was no dividing wall between the hearth area and the main bedroom, just a pony wall, its edges curved at the ceiling. Beyond was the larger section of the room, with a luxurious four-poster bed. In the gloom, he could make out that it was enclosed by heavy curtains. He would have to pull them back to find out whether she was in there or not. Or… he could stand close and listen.

He noticed the door to the bathroom – beside the fire, where she'd been when he'd called out to her – was also open. He moved in front of the fire, glancing up at the painting, a modern portrait of a proud woman in a riding outfit, boots, white jodhpurs and navy tunic. She had a whip in her hand but wasn't wearing a helmet, her dark hair tied behind her head. A striking-looking character, for sure.

He peered around the edge of the open door, saw the infeasibly large bathroom, its floorboards lit dimly by pale moonlight. A clawfoot bath with a bevelled edge stood against the wall opposite the window.

There was no one in there. He turned and walked towards the bed, listening carefully with each step, hoping to hear breathing, perhaps a light, alcohol-induced snore. Away from the fire, the room was much darker, but his vision adjusted as he went. He could make out the fanned curtains on the windows, some sort of dark stain on the floor – a rug, presumably – and the four-poster bed itself, huge, bigger than his van in fact. Some people had the money…

He reached the corner of the bed, stopped. Ticking. He could hear the ticking of a clock, perhaps the one he'd heard coming up the stairs? Although he didn't think so, it wasn't loud enough to be heard outside the room, surely.

Nothing else.

He held his breath, to try and catch even the faintest sound. The murmur of air through a parched mouth. There was nothing.

He reached up and stroked his fingers along the curtain, seeking the break where he could peek in. Should he say something out loud? He'd scare the life out of her if she was there and woke to see someone standing over her. She'd think he was the Old Man of the Black or something equally horrific.

But then again, saying something might scare her too. At least if he was quiet and she turned out to be in there, he had a chance of leaving her sound asleep.

A sudden pop made him spin around, terrified.

Only an ember in the fire, he reassured himself. After taking a few slow, deep breaths to calm his thumping heart, he turned back and felt along the curtain, the dense weave of the cotton. It was only when he reached the darkened corner, where there was no light at all, that he found the edge. Holding his breath again, he eased it back and leaned forward so his head was inside.

There was no light and, after a second, he realised no noise either – except for the muted tick.

He drew his phone from his pocket, and squeezed a button to provide a faint glow. Directed it across the covers, piled pillows, the unslept-in bed.

59.

He let out a long sigh.

He'd been more tense pulling the curtain back than he'd realised. He needed to relax. Just this lunchtime he'd been listening to some health guru on a talk show, saying how you couldn't control the things that happened to you, only how you reacted to them. So, here he was, stranded in a remote, haunted house, his only companion a stranger – albeit one with whom he'd quickly formed a strong bond – who had vanished. Any moment one of those ghosts could reappear.

So what could he do? How could he control the situation, manage his emotions, this impossible anxiety?

He could control it simply because he had to. It was the *only* thing he could do, the only option. So he would. What was the worst that could happen?

Breathe in through the nose, out through the mouth. Four times. Five. That's what the guy on the radio had suggested. As he did so, he felt his thoughts slowing down, his broad body standing there, steady, in the darkness by the bed. He was a solid man, and he was taking stock.

Right. So Rose wasn't here. Where else might she be? He had to search the rest of the house. Room by room. There was no way he would be going to sleep anyway, not tonight. Sleep – what a joke!

He walked back towards the hearth, towards the double doors. He would head down the dark corridor, or perhaps along the gallery, where he'd seen the girl. Search the house.

That was what he was going to do. Search the whole house until he found her.

As he reached the armchair, he glanced at the portrait above the stone mantelpiece.

The rider, she was an attractive woman. Those boots, the jodhpurs. Sexy, he thought. Very sexy. What was that Netflix series again? And her skin, lovely, white and clear, with a proud mouth. All no doubt enhanced by the artist. She was looking down on you, ever so slightly. Superior, but hiding it. *Most* of it, wanting to let a little bit through, just so you knew.

And then he noticed something about the portrait. Above her head, to his right, there was a dark smudge. The light was poor, he squinted to see better, because it was bigger than he'd realised, it had a strange luminous quality about it. He dug in his pocket for his phone, began to draw it out when…

60.

The woman's head was obliterated by a viscous black swirl, like a horrible oil, frothing and twisting, smothering more and more of the portrait and then, as Ryan watched, stunned, it began to break up from the middle outwards as something pale and misshapen like bone, no, a nose and cheek, an open mouth, chin, then closed eyes, black eyebrows, dark, wet-looking hair, a woman's face came squeezing out and only subliminally did he notice the clunk as his hand released his phone and it hit the floor and then there was a whole head, thrusting itself from the womb-like blackness like a demon, desperate, features knotted with anguish, bursting forth, followed by white shoulders, a thin, angular arm, elbow striking at the air, long fingers raking in front of the picture, nails coming towards him –

…and with a splashing of liquid the woman slipped from the despicable rupture and was floating there, dressed in grey in front of him, her mouth open inches from his, her white teeth a fraction apart from his, eyes wide, black and furious as they stared into his own, and then…

She screamed.

61.

It was a sound like nothing on earth.

It sliced his ears, pierced his brain with long needles, whipped his neck and diced his guts with dagger-sharp nails. Hellish images bombarded him, the torture and pain of living creatures, filling him with terror and things even worse, despair, the loneliest, most desolate moments of his life all smashed into one, nothing worth staying for, everything was lost, gone, there was nothing to fight for, all he could do was get away, run, but there was nowhere to go, no corner to hide in ever again, he was so scared, bewildered and confused, something hard and evil was exposed in his soul, he had to get away from those staring mad eyes, the frenzy, he had to…

He keeled over backward and his head struck something hard.

62.

Blurred dark.

A smell, near the back of the throat.

A favourite smell, but not now, so acrid.

Smoke. The reek of woodsmoke. Old woodsmoke.

He blinked. There was something hard, an edge, corner, right above him. But it was so dark. He couldn't focus.

Something solid, dependable. Something that stayed stable. The edge of something – a table.

There was only grey light and this hard edge above his eyes, which wouldn't stay still. Was it moving?

No. His sight. Like seeing through old, warped glass.

A movement, somewhere peripheral. He sought it out, moving his head. Apprehending faint greyness, then thicker grey, something there.

Coming up to him. Something smudged but most definite, defined, like a big cannister or barrel or tree trunk. All those things it wasn't. Blurred and dark. Blue. Dark blue.

It was a leg, that's what it was, he felt a shiver of joy, the joy of recognition. Comprehension. Perception. Correct understanding. There was a leg.

And a leg meant a person.

Yes, he was getting it now, things were falling into place, the angles were making it hard but there was a stomach above, a large chest – breasts – above that, and then a chin, a face, a woman's face, with hair close to her head.

'Ryan.'

He heard another sound, an *aaah* sound, struggling, groaning, indefinite. Like Marjorie Taylor's son, in his chair. Marjorie Taylor? Realised it might be himself, he might be making that noise.

And then, he remembered.

Remembered the woman screaming.

63.

He sat up with a sharp intake of breath, only just avoiding clouting his head on the table.

Looked in fear at the picture hanging above the grey fireplace, his arm coming up instinctively to protect himself.

The painting remained dark, shaded. Inert.

'Shit!' he shouted.

Still on the floor, he twisted, searching the gloom for the ghost. The screaming woman. The bean nighe, as Rose had called her…

There was nothing there. Nothing that he could see, at least.

He sprang to his feet – or rather, intended to spring to his feet, but found his body, or brain, would only let him come up slowly, gripping the table for support. He was groggy, he realised. Groggy from drink, from falling down – had he been unconscious for a moment? – and groggy from too much terror.

Who was that woman?

On his feet, he stumbled to the door, found the light switch, flipped it down.

The room appeared in all its magnitude, lit by a half dozen mellow sconces. Shaped like flame, like those in the corridor outside.

Ryan twisted around, making sure he was not about to be scared out of his mind once more by some dark, materialising vision.

All remained stable. He raised his wrist to his mouth, clamped his teeth against it. Steadied his breathing. That woman…

He'd never seen or heard anything so awful in his life. That scream, the pitch, if a noise could have killed him, that was surely it. And not just with fear but with bleakness, a soul destroying desolation…

He stood, staring at the floor, remembering the barrage of feelings as she… as she what?… *assaulted* him with that noise. The hollowness, the compounded misery of a life, of all life, lost in a hard place, the despair, no hope at all, a memory of something in childhood, two friends taking his Dinky toy car, shoving him to the ground and storming off, his mother not there, it was that, plus the heartbreak of seeing Patty, his first love, snogging Jon Pratt, at the boat club disco, and *every* other bad feeling he'd ever had, all crushed into one…

He shoved the thought aside, unable to deal with it. Too much emotion, he couldn't…

And then remembered something else.

Something as he'd come round, out of the blackness of his unconsciousness, the temporary oblivion.

The woman. Standing above him.

Isla, again.

64.

What was she doing, standing over him like that?

And also, in his dream earlier? In the corner of the living room, watching the scene, watching the family and… him.

How…?

He felt the ground shift, like when he'd been on a ship a few years back, sailing to Ireland, a storm, they'd been hit by large waves and then a giant one, it pushed the deck to a terrible pitch, over forty-five degrees (he was sure now it couldn't have been), how could they not go under with such force, all the glasses smashing, people staggering, tables and chairs sliding away…

It was like that now, his whole sense of gravity gone, because, if he was seeing his sister here, like this, in this place of ghosts…

Was she dead?

65.

He stumbled, reached out to stop himself falling, caught hold of the armchair, swung himself around, collapsed into it, uncaring of the imperious gaze of the woman staring down at him.

Let her come back if she wanted to. What did he care?

His sister, dead. His beloved sister.

Had she finally passed away, after months in her coma bed? Slipped into the cold night, appeared at the edge of his vision, of his half dreaming mind, to pass on one last morsel of care, love, to let him know she was gone?

'Shut up, Ryan.' He said it aloud, head in hands. 'Shut up!'

He didn't know. Didn't know she was dead. He was speculating. Probably hallucinating. And if he was hallucinating her, might he be hallucinating all of this? The whole damned thing? Had he made his final drop of the day to Ashcraig, headed back through the snow to Newton, gone out for beers with his mates and then gone home to bed, all as planned? Was this – he looked around at the dull fire, the gothic archway to the bathroom, the woman in the portrait – was this all a dream?

He could only hope. It was the only way it would make sense.

'God...' He pinched the skin on the back of his hand.

There was no way of telling. Every minute here had a hallucinatory quality – from the moment he arrived, before that even, the snowball hitting the window – all of it was, to a lesser or greater extent, surreal. Utterly surreal.

But, at the same time, it all *felt* real. The seconds ticked by with that unseen clock. There was no hurrying this, not like a dream.

No, he had to face it. Unbelievable as it was, he had to carry on as if it was all real.

He stifled a sob.

'So... if it's true, sis, if all of this is bloody real... are you dead?'

66.

He looked around, smelling the smoky ash of the fire, seeing the large room, a picture of a mountain, a photo of some misty loch between the windows, another abstract on the opposite wall, greys, blues, pinks.

Silence reigned.

'OK, just for now, just because... I can't stand it, not on top of everything else, if you are –' he sniffed, '– I'm going to assume you're not. You're not dead, sis, you're just a figment of my disintegrating mind, my screwed imagination.'

He blinked tears from his eyes. Sniffed in deeply again, straightened his back.

'And now, I'm going to find Rose. Find out what's happened to her, where she went. And then we're going to get out of this bloody place, walk for a few hours in a bloody blizzard if we have to, but we're going to get to the neighbours, the farmer, whoever it is lives down the road, and we're going to spend the rest of the night with them.'

He looked around once more, glanced up at the painting. The painting that didn't change.

'Alright, sis?'

After a pause, he stood up and walked out of the room.

67.

'Rose!'

He stood in the gallery and shouted her name.

'Rose!'

He had to start acting, to keep ahead of his debilitating fear, of a terror that was literally making him shake at the knees, turning his legs to jelly. To hell with those ghosts.

There was no reply, just the quiet of the house. Or rather, the return of those noises you don't normally heed, the click of pipes, fitted joints, the faint ticking of the clock. He strode down the landing with the evenly spaced doors, down towards the southern, portcullis end of the house. The first door, arched like the others, was shut. He pushed down the handle, eased it open and flicked on the lights.

It was, as expected, a bedroom. From the clutter, the navy-and-white spaceship quilt, the diagrams of planets, Transformers and football posters, a boy's room. And there were clocks, several of them, antique clocks in wooden cases, watches on the desk and side table, a plastic pendulum clock on the wall with a small hatch at the top, a cuckoo clock. Now he knew where the ticking had come from. The windows had been hung around with fairy lights, which had been left on, and there was a tiny Christmas tree on the windowsill. There was a built-in closet he didn't bother checking.

The next room had a double bed and appeared to be for an older occupant. There was a sleek laptop on the desk, a white iMac, art prints on the walls, dark throws on a two-seater couch beneath the window. A TV was fixed by a bracket above the desk, watchable from the sofa and bed. He spotted a ring-bound notebook on the bedside table and went to check it.

The pictures on the cover were more juvenile than he'd expected, drawings of hearts and a cartoon dog, Bluey, he thought, from the Australian kids' programme. He watched it sometimes, hanging out at his friend Juliet's maisonette, with her little boy, Gavin. There were seagulls too, in the same style. He lifted the book and opened the first page. Contact details were completed in a neat script, Georgina Leslie, with phone, home address and a promise to reward the return of the journal with a £20 payment.

He flicked through the pages. In looping blue ballpoint pen, there were dated descriptions of places visited, coffee shops, Edinburgh castle for Hogmanay, a weekend trip to New York with her mother, a holiday to Sweden. There was something recently about a boy she fancied who lived nearby. *If only Josh's dad weren't such a PIG,* he read, towards the end of the filled pages, halfway through the book. The last entry was dated 21st December, describing a day indoors because of the weather, unable to see Josh, a day of *indescribable boredom, bored, bored, BORED BORED!!!* It ended:

Tomorrow going to Glasgow for our usual overnighter with dad and my brothers. Will get something special for Josh, maybe a Korn T-shirt if I can find one (although think they might only be available online?). Still can't believe what he said in that email. Persuade Rose to take it round to him, she gets on with the Ridleys.

He thought about Rose. He could imagine her getting on with people, she was the type. Confident but with a hidden, oddly appealing, vulnerability. Where was she?

Ryan put the journal down and checked the ensuite, with its vanity mirror circled by bulbs and shampoo and lotion bottles stacked untidily along the top of the bath.

He returned to the landing. He was nearing the gloomy end of the corridor, but he found another switch, which lit all the way to the end. He came to the final door on the right, another bedroom, this one clearly that of a younger child. There was a raised single bed with safety rail, a scattering of plastic toys on the floor, and a hand-painted mural depicting Peter Pan flying Wendy and her brothers from the window of their London town house with the help of Tinker Bell.

What was the name of the third child Rose had mentioned? His head still throbbing from adrenalin and drink, he couldn't remember again. He'd just had it, hadn't he? ... C-, C-, Coran, that was it...

At the end of the corridor, he found another, smaller door on the left-hand wall. He realised he was walking above the carport so, if he'd got it right, this was a door out on to… what? There were no rooms above the entrance gate. He turned the wrought-iron handle and shoved, but it didn't budge. There was a key in the door, which he hadn't noticed because even with the lights it was dark down this end.

He turned the key and tried the door again.

68.

It opened, on to the freezing night.

Outside, there was a narrow walkway connecting the two wings of the manor, squaring off the building footprint. It ran directly over the top of the portcullis gate. The temperature was shockingly cold and there was a light wind but still he stepped out and stood up at the parapet wall. He pulled down his shirt sleeves and buttoned the cuffs, then wrapped his arms around his sides to retain a little of the heat of the house.

He needed this after the claustrophobia of indoors – the good, cold air would clear his head. And the view in the moonlight was awesome.

Below, the black avenue of stretched, leafless limes snaked away towards the road. Around them was the snow-levelled sweep of open lawn, punctuated by singular trees, skeletal, mushrooming oaks, and dark, tapering pines. The top of one of the pines fronting the house was only a few feet away from him, its branches weighted with snow.

But most impressive were the fields in the distance, with a small farm and, visible now the blizzard had stopped, rolling mountains beyond, their smooth slopes overlapping like a sculpture in ice.

Ryan leaned into the cold wall, absorbing the scene. His homeland, his Scotland, it was just so damned… beautiful.

He heard something, a muffled thump, and felt something cold splash on his cheek. He wiped it away, water. Melted snow. He looked up at the star-pricked sky, but it was clear. There was another thud below him, but no splash this time, just flecks of white flying up above the parapet, then falling back down.

He looked over the edge. Felt his skin shrink against his bones, all over, as he spotted a figure on the lawn below, fringed in shivering black.

69.

It was a boy, a boy in a thick winter coat, a parka with the hood up. He was bending down through his own throbbing inkiness to scoop up more snow with mittened fingers.

Ryan didn't wait. Struck with panic, he ran back into the house, slamming the parapet door and sprinting up the landing, back towards Rose's bedroom.

At the top of the stairs he paused, hearing more thumping, coming from the steps below the half landing, the section out of sight.

'Rose?' he said.

There was another strike, followed by a lighter scuffing, surely feet on the stairs.

'Rose!' he cried, grasping the wall and holding his breath, listening. 'Is that you?'

Another thump.

Then the squeezing in his temples, the insufferable pressure of dread as another step was taken, surely about to reach the turn – and he was off again, running down the long gallery, knowing, knowing with all his being, that whoever – whatever – was coming up those stairs…

It was not Rose.

70.

The gallery was long.

On his left were oil paintings – landscapes, sporting prints, abstracts, portraits – which he barely took in as he ran past Rose's room, on towards the end. On his right were long, latticed windows overlooking the courtyard, more oils filling the narrow gaps between them.

As he reached the halfway point he stopped, skidding slightly on the runner, as a girl stood before him.

A girl with thick, chestnut hair, the fringe held back by a pink band, her nose long, thin, eyes set close together. A girl in a flouncy white dress, surrounded by an ebony blotting of the air, reminiscent of a photographic negative. She was staring at Ryan with those small, narrow eyes, staring with disbelief, and with malice.

He stared back, the flow of time ceasing with morbid fascination, like a mice swiped down by some dreadful feline's paw, awaiting the killing blow.

As he stared the girl stopped looking angry and a furrow appeared on her forehead, above her eyebrows which were starting to jerk up and down. Her eyes swayed away from his as if she was losing her sense of balance, looking for a fixed point. Her shoulders rose and fell and her hand came up to her mouth, her chest convulsing with a sudden belch. She began to look worried, to turn away from him, as if… *embarrassed.*

And then, as Ryan watched in horror, the girl's mouth opened and a foul, dark liquid began to spill from her lips and down her chin, then she retched and more spewed out to splash on the floor. She looked up, saw Ryan as if for the first time, and reached out for him, a look of bewilderment, of shock and horror, on her face…

He gasped, a strangled sound – smelling the stench of the girl, the vomit, at the back of his throat – then lunged left, in the gap between her and the wall. His shoulder struck a painting, a large Dutch landscape with windmills, which tilted sharply but didn't fall.

Then he was screaming, and running again, towards the far end of the landing.

71.

At the end of the gallery, there were doors to left and right. He flung open the left one, sure to be another bedroom, desperate for somewhere to seal himself away from the ghouls.

He was right. Switching on the lights, he saw another grand room similar to Rose and Peter's, with a fireplace and sprawling queen-sized bed. There was an ensuite and what he assumed was a built-in wardrobe.

He took all this in in seconds, his mind racing with where to go, how to protect himself from the horrors outside. On impulse, he darted through to the bathroom and locked the door behind him. Switching on the light, he pressed his back against the door, breathing heavily.

Like Shelley Duvall in *The* bloody *Shining*, he thought, clamping his eyes shut for a moment, trying to break the crazy merry-go-round of panic in his head.

'Ridiculous, bloody ridiculous…' he muttered. In his mind's eye, the boy and girl were already in the bedroom, stepping in exaggerated, mechanised fashion towards the bathroom door.

'Stop it!' he hissed. He had to rid himself of these debilitating images. He was safe, he had to tell himself he was safe here. They didn't know he was here, did they even think, work things out?

'Oh God,' he muttered. He needed to think of something else, something to clear this miasma of terror.

Then he had it.

He pictured her in his mind's eye, standing there, by that bath with its rolled top, standing and smiling at him, that dimply little smile with the wrinkly pinches at the corner of her hazel eyes.

Isla. He conjured Isla before him, just like he had twice before this evening.

His beautiful, calm, wise sister.

Isla.

72.

'Help me, sis,' he said, realising he was crying again. 'I don't know how much more of this I can take...'

She smiled, just a few steps away from him. Her mouth opened, her small mouth, he used to call her *button chops* when they were kids, teasing her. He leaned forward, keeping pressure on the door – an absurd notion in his head that if he turned he might see them, if he held hard he'd stop them breaking through – and strained to hear her.

Because she *was* talking. Isla was speaking to him.

It's just... he couldn't hear what she was saying.

'What is it, sis?' he asked. Then: 'No – no, Isla, don't leave me!'

But there was nothing he could do. She faded as he watched, her mouth seeming to vanish last, still speaking to him, saying... what?

'You'd better not be dead,' he said, stupidly.

He looked around at the room, seeing a metal razor and foam on the sink, an electric toothbrush, a black can of spray deodorant. It was a man's bathroom, he realised. He recognised the woody musk of the shaving foam, possibly compounded with aftershave. Plus there was something else in there, something more... acrid? Sour?

He sniffed. Just a hint of something rank.

He looked at the lavish sink, with its bronze taps capped with a ceramic C and H. He could see a few matt patches on the porcelain, either toothpaste or the shave foam, not properly rinsed. And there was something else, a few spattered patches of brown, here and there a yellow tinge. Beige blobs, like little whiteheads.

What was it?

He realised his anxiety was easing. The image of Isla, the distraction of the sink, had settled his nerves. The ghosts had not come through the door. Maybe they were still there, but if so they were biding their time. He shivered. Stepped away from the door, peered more closely at the sink.

As he did so, the sour odour increased. He wrinkled his nose. It was rank.

He turned away. On top of his anxiety and hangover, the smell was making him feel sick.

He faced the door. He couldn't stay in here forever. He was going to have to go back out.

With a shake of his head, he stepped forward, reached for the knob. As soon as he touched it he let go and took two steps back. Scratched his neck.

'Come on.'

He stepped forward, lifted his hand. Froze again.

'Shit!'

He rushed the door, twisted the lock, and flung it open.

73.

There was no one there – nothing there.

He listened, but this time there was no sound in the house. No creaking of pipes or floorboards, no wind rattling the casements, no settling of unseen beams. Nothing. Just deathly silence.

He had a thought then, about Rose, had she just abandoned him? Woken up beside him on the couch, realised she'd betrayed her husband and family, and run off into the night? Maybe she'd decided to make her way to the Ridley's farm.

After all, he barely knew her. What might she do?

Somehow, he couldn't buy it. Their connection… it had been so strong. The desire. Passion. Surely she felt it too? She wouldn't leave him like that.

In which case... what?

Had she had an accident? Fallen on the stairs? Or perhaps when she'd left him, gone elsewhere in the house, she'd found one of *them* again, been scared witless, fallen in shock? Maybe she was passed out somewhere? Or worse...

He couldn't countenance that idea. Not after the shock of seeing Isla's... *spirit*.

He had to double down, find Rose. He'd been through most the house now, there was just the eastern wing, which must have a fair portion taken up with the second storey of the library in the tower. He was going to do it, he was going to get through that last bit and then, damn it, he was going to get out of here, walk out if he had to, put on his coat and take his chances with the freeze. It couldn't be that far to the farm, it couldn't even be that long until early morning, it must be well past four or even five a.m. now, surely? The prospect of daylight quickened his heartbeat, for once with hope not fear.

As he strode towards the door something caught his eye on the bedside table, lit by the fringed sidelamp.

There was a book and beside that a set of keys, with something that looked distinctly like a fob.

He stopped and walked over to it.

It was a key fob, attached to the other keys on the ring. He picked it up, held the chrome edge to the lamplight, saw the embossed lettering on the edge.

RANGE ROVER.

74.

As he headed out, he was thinking, maybe they no longer sleep together, if their relationship has got that bad? That's why they each have a master bedroom. He found the thought first gratifying, then depressing when he realised he was lusting after a woman in distress, a *married* woman in distress…

Rose evidently hadn't checked Peter's room when she was searching for the key. So all he had to do now was find her and they could escape together in the car, safe against the freezing night. He was sure he could navigate the flooded brook – maybe would even try the hill again, he was full of confidence. He clutched the fob tightly in his pocket as he walked.

Even so, he paused as he came back out into the long gallery, looking carefully down the hall to see if there was any sign of the girl. There wasn't, so he hurried to the double doors at the eastern end. They were open, so he went through into an antechamber filled with military paraphernalia – axes, guns and knives on the walls, a second suit of plate armour in the far corner, and a large, internally-lit display cabinet on the lefthand wall. He paused briefly to look at the display.

It was filled with medals pinned to a sloping board covered in white cloth. Each had a small interpretative card beneath it, naming the medal and the conditions under which it would be awarded. A few had larger cards, those for which the particulars of the award were known. A Corporal killed at Ypres, returning a vital radio to his line; a Major blown up in Afghanistan, defusing an IED; the tragedies of a murderous, inglorious world wishing not to forget its moments of surpassing loyalty.

Like most of his mates, Ryan took more than a passing interest in warfare. He would have liked to examine the medals and this makeshift armoury in more detail – but of course he couldn't. With a glance behind to check there were no spirits breaking out from the Black, he hurried to the next set of doors, which were shut. He was sure these would lead into the library.

As he was about to push the handles, he was distracted by something above the arch of the doorway. Or rather, an absence above it. In a prominent position, two hooks were screwed into the wall – two hooks that should have held something, like all the other fixtures in the room – but instead held nothing.

He paused. What would they have displayed? Possibly a sword, or an axe, or even something longer, like a halberd. Maybe a musket, or a rifle. Anything, in fact.

There was no working it out, he realised, as he reached to pull open the doors.

75.

He was right. It was the library.

He switched on the lights and examined the gallery and the bare walls and narrow windows of the tower, rising thirty feet or so above. The mezzanine here was a good ten foot wide, with two separate reading areas, one with an armchair and lamplit side table adjacent to the tall window, the other with two small couches facing one another, a fringed standing lamp between them. The walls were lined top to bottom with books old and new, a quick glance revealing modern biographies of politicians, Blair, Cameron, Obama, the next shelf poetry by Auden, Longfellow, Eliot. There was a copy of Donna Tartt's *The Secret History* with its black spine, out of place amid the poets. As he looked he spotted more books breaking the themes, books on disability issues, science, the environment. A hint of chaos amidst the order.

He noticed a leatherbound book placed on the backrest of the nearest couch. He went over and picked it up.

Things of the Night, was printed in capitalised gold on the red leather spine. He opened the title page, saw it was written by a woman, Connie May. He remembered what Rose had told him about this great grandparent of Peter's, the spiritualist. He flicked through the pages, saw a quote from Hamlet – *Thou com'st in such a questionable shape, That I will speak to thee!* – chapters on Haunted Dwellings, The Medium, Apparitions of the Night.

It was as he flicked through this last chapter that he noticed a reference to Ectoplasm – a *Slime like a Woodland Mould that erupts when a Fresh Spirit emerges from the Night*. Yeah, that pretty much describes it, he thought. He would have read more, wondered if perhaps he could find something more about the bean nighe either in the book or elsewhere in the library, but realised he needed to get on, get out. He was still hoping to find Rose, but the emptiness of the library was increasingly making him think something else must have happened. It was unlikely she'd fallen and knocked herself out, he hadn't searched every cranny and closet but what were the chances she would have crawled away somewhere and passed out? Vanishingly small. Perhaps he was right about her running away, she'd become disturbed, either by what happened with him or the ghosts, and disappeared into the snowstorm. He thought about those scars on her arms. Had they been self-harm, even worse, an attempt to kill herself?

He shuddered. 'Can't think about it now, sis,' he muttered. He needed to focus on getting out. He could come back with help – as soon as he found it.

The gallery formed a U-shape above the lower library, the stairs emerging in the middle section ahead of him. As he drew near to them, he looked over the balcony and saw the things he'd first seen from the outside when he was waiting to be let in – the armchair near the fire, a book open on the table beside it, the Christmas tree, Persian rug.

And then, as he stared down, he noticed something else.

The faintest sound… a tapping.

He froze, listening.

Nothing. Although then, a measured metallic ping, surely the radiator pipes.

Maybe that was what he'd heard. Or just the old wood, the beams stretching and contracting again, like the bones of some old giant.

He began to descend to the lower floor.

76.

Ectoplasm.

A disgusting concept, he thought, as he came down into the lower library, lit by the lamp beside the leather armchair, the muted glow of the Christmas tree, and the fire – which was still burning surprisingly well. At the far end of the room, near the windows, he could see a large desk with an unlit lamp. He imagined Peter Leslie, the world famous poet, sitting there, wrestling with his lines and metre.

Ghost splatter. Foul…

He shook his head, scarcely able to believe his night so far, thinking back to his decision twelve hours' ago to push on and make the delivery. What a fool. But then, if he hadn't done all that, he would never have met… *her*.

He looked around for a light switch, for any sign of Rose in the dimness of the room.

'Rose!' he shouted. Silence. He noticed the blackness of the windows on to the courtyard where he knew the Toyota stood silent, with its covering of snow. Fingered the smooth fob of the Range Rover in his pocket.

He sighed. He'd done his best. It was time to go. Leave the terror of this hellhole behind him. He would just have to come back with help to find Rose – with the police? What would he say to them? He could hardly tell them the truth, they'd have him bloody sectioned…

He made his way towards the door to the downstairs hall, which would take him back to the living room.

And stopped.

There it was again.

Tap…tap…tap, tap…tap…

It was louder down here, a little arrhythmic like the pipes but… more hollow, bass-like than the pipes, more even than the easing of wood. A distant knocking.

He stared around in the gloom, into the dark crevices by the fireplace, across at the Christmas tree hung with baubles and tinsel and fairy lights, up at the tall, shadowy shelves of books. What was it?

'Rose…?' he said again, his voice cracking as his nerves again took hold. 'Is that you?'

It seemed to be coming from somewhere beneath the staircase, a place filled with purpose-built slanted shelves, crammed with even more books. The library of a great book lover, of a renowned *man of letters*, wasn't that what they called them?

As he approached the darkened shelves the noise ceased. He stood, waiting in the shadows, eyes scanning the dim corner, hoping it would sound again, give him an idea of what might be causing it. He had a vague notion in his head, a half-remembered film, in which someone beat pipes to alert others of their presence. The noise could travel far, couldn't it, down a long pipe? Was Rose somewhere else in the house, tapping a radiator, maybe upstairs, or in an adjacent room? The hallway, between the library and the living room? That was now the only place he hadn't been…

The silence lasted, until he became aware of another sound, the accelerating thrash of blood in his ears.

No, it was time to go. Check the downstairs gallery and that was it. Even though he realised Rose could have moved around as he did, his nerves couldn't take another tour of the whole house just on this faintest of possibilities.

He was going.

Except, as he turned back towards the door, the air began to spatter with ghastly, unearthly Black once again.

77.

The light of the tree frayed and smudged as the Old Man's painfully creased face began to break through the coal-like membrane, to shove itself back at the cowering man.

Ryan's gut weakened, his legs began to shake. White light, a blinding terror, flashed in his head. Putrid liquid spilled from the edges of the man's wrestling body, making Ryan retch, fight back vomit.

Get out, get out – the words raced through his head.

He stumbled to the side, seeing those eyes shivering in the air, shaking, like they would if the man was riding a fairground attraction, a wild, careening rollercoaster. The stuff of nightmares, made real.

Run, you idiot, he thought, but he was no longer in control of his buckling legs. He stumbled against the table by the armchair, bashing it over, as the man's elegantly dressed torso lunged out at him. He heard a snarl, felt something wet slap his face. He wiped it away, imagining the foul substance of the ectoplasm.

He had to run.

But, as he dodged the materialising apparition, a sense of asymmetry, of incompleteness, dogged him. Something was wrong. He sucked in air, needing something, oxygen, to sustain something, *thought*, he needed to see what was wrong, what was different, to give himself, his power of reason, a sliver of energy, the window of opportunity, so he could observe the old figure before him and realise that…

He was not being threatened.

Because the man, the Old Man of the Black, had stopped, stopped squirming out from the Black, stopped convulsing towards Ryan with all that anger and pain on his face…

And he was swinging his open palm, as if gesturing.

78.

Time froze.

Slowly, Ryan turned his head in the direction of the man's waving hand.

The adrenaline, terror, blood, they all seemed to slow, to thicken in his veins. He knew he was on the verge, about to see something that would change his whole world, harrow him for eternity, set him free, turn him mad, destroy him in an instant.

Something was coming.

Ryan looked to where the Old Man of the Black was pointing.

IV.

The Room

79.

Ryan frowned.

All he saw was where he had just been. The darkened bookshelves, beneath the staircase banisters.

He looked back at the man, saw a new expression on his face, eyebrows raised, eyes steady, glaring. Wet, but not with ectoplasm…

And then he heard it again – the knocking.

Tap, tap…tap…tap…

He could do one of two things. He could run, easily the safest option – or he could go back to that bookshelf and… what then?

Ryan forced himself to regard the man, his ebony halo, his shroud of greasy soot. The ghost. He was dressed in a suit, light blue, and wearing a neat brown tie. He was, in fact, dapper. *Hint of a chuckle, deep down, a ghost – dapper... for real?* His lined face was sorrowful, his hair half-grey, half-brown. There were tears at the corners of his eyes, forming lines down his cheeks. Ryan could see all this because the man cast a muted, unearthly glow about him.

The man was upset.

He had been angry. But now he was sad.

Ryan knew he should run. But somehow, struggling on shock-weakened legs, he returned to the bookshelf.

80.

As he stood there, he heard the sound again, the tapping.

He pressed his ear against the books and it became louder. Reaching into his pocket, he brought out his phone and switched on the torch, all the time taking short, brief breaths, feeling as if his diaphragm had risen and was stuck an inch from his throat.

The torch revealed old, antique books, brown and navy leather spines. His gaze flitted across titles, *The Book of Knowledge, The World's Great Events, Italian Opera...* There was nothing here, too much here, to take in.

'What do you want?' he said, turning back, shocked – sick and shocked – to see the face right behind him, to smell sourness in the air, a rancid smell he recognised, from this house somewhere, from the ensuite bathroom, the smell in the sink…

'What?' he cried.

Then followed the man's gaze down to a lower section of the shelf, redirecting his torch to a gap in the books, to a slender handle he would never have seen…

Ryan looked back into the old man's face, felt his jaw go slack so close to something so unnatural, something so unbelievable, out of this world, yet something so…

Human.

He turned back and lifted the handle, pulling hard, once, twice, before the whole artificial bookcase swung toward him, exposing a space in greater darkness beyond.

81.

He raised his torch, intending to point it into the hidden area, but his instincts told him of more change, something in the light, he glanced back at the Old Man but…

He was no longer there.

The Old Man of the Black had gone.

Once more, Ryan felt himself alone.

He took another deep breath, lifted the torch with his shaking hand, and peered around the edge of the shelf, giddy with dread.

'Hello…' he said. 'Rose?'

He breathed in sharply, astonished, bewildered, at what he saw. There was a leg, a human leg in jeans, on the floor.

'Shit!'

He forced himself to look around the unlit chamber, swinging the torch.

And froze, trying to make sense of what was in front of him, to take in what was… incomprehensible.

Completely incomprehensible.

82.

Bodies. Human bodies.

Limbs, torsos, hands, all intertwined with each other. All slack, white, pale in the torchlight, lacking in colour, rigidity, lacking in… life.

'Oh… my…' he whispered. His skin was crawling again, he yelled, an eruption of primal terror…

And then he was breaking through the shower of panic, forcing himself to focus again, because there was something…

Within the limbs, the man, the girl, the boy's face staring upwards with nothing but a rictus grin… there was something moving.

Scarcely able to breath, breathing too sharp, he didn't know anymore what was happening, he flashed the light around and there, amidst the girl in the white dress, arm across forehead, the boy in the parka, the dead woman with dark hair – Rose, was it Rose? he wasn't sure, *oh* – there was another person, a smaller boy, propped on a man in a suit, neck bent awkwardly against the slope of the staircase, arm outstretched, knuckles moving up and down against the wooden panel…

The boy who had been knocking.

The boy who, amidst all this horrific death, was alive.

And then, as Ryan's reason returned, as he crouched down, preparing to move into the chamber, to help the boy, to help Rose, *surely it wasn't Rose, it couldn't be her?* something, someone else appeared before him, a flash, an image in his mind, nothing more, surely, but something, yes, the eyes, warm, hazel, the bobbed hair, small 'O' of a mouth, his sister, Isla, there before him, crouched too, in the space, and she was speaking, saying something to him, but this time it was different, different because, yes, he heard, actually heard what she said, which was…

Turn around.

83.

He turned.

And dived sideways, behind the nearby chair, as a figure beside the tree discharged a shotgun at him.

On all fours he gasped, staring in disbelief at the carpet.

Then a noise, a scraping as something was knocked, as the person moved in the room – surely, coming round to shoot him behind the chair!

He scrambled around it, towards the fire, as the air was shattered by another mighty crack. He felt a sting at the back of his thighs and cried out in pain.

'God!'

He leapt up, circled round the chair, because the two shots, both barrels of the gun, had been fired and because…

He needed to face his assailant.

84.

'Rose…'

She was standing there, a few feet away, in her flowery dress, the gun slack at her side.

'What the hell…?'

Hadn't he just seen her, her crumpled body in the hidden room? How was she here?

'What are you doing?' he said. The backs of his thighs felt like they were burning.

Rose slumped against the side of the armchair. She released the gun and it clattered on the floor.

'It's me, Rose,' he said. 'Ryan…' All he could think was she'd been hunted by whoever – whatever – had killed those people, and now mistaken him for a threat. Her expression, her eyes drifting a little above his head, towards the uppermost part of the tower, her mouth open – it frightened him.

'What happened?' he asked. He took a step towards her, his hands outstretched in front of him.

She turned her head slowly from side to side, making a sound through her mouth – a quiet, strangled groan. She became blurred. Ryan shook his head, trying to clear his vision. He knew about shock, he was going into shock…

He thought about Isla.

'Rose, speak to me,' he said, forcing himself to concentrate. He took another step towards her. His legs hurt, but the pain was bearable. 'Who are they? Who are all those people under there?'

She said something, a word, but it was unclear because she continued making the sorrowful groaning noise, from the base of her throat.

'What?' he said.

'Dead,' she said.

'How did they die? Do you know?' He was nearly with her now.

She looked at him askance, her head still tilted upwards as if in awe, prayer, or transcendent grief. Then she whispered:

'I killed them. It was me.'

85.

'What?'

'I wanted you to go… leave without me. But you wouldn't.'

He stopped a couple of paces from her.

'You did what?' he asked again. He couldn't believe it, couldn't believe he'd heard right.

'He gave her everything… he never did with me.' She lowered her head and looked in his eyes. 'So I took it all away from them.'

Ryan grasped his brow, shook his head. Looked back at her. 'You're telling me you've killed them? Is it Peter and… who?' He thought then of the boy, the one who was knocking, who was still alive. Maybe some of the others were, too?

'His wife, Rose. And his children.'

Ryan gasped, trying to take it in, trying to breathe. 'You're his wife…' he muttered.

'Ex-wife. Second of three. My name's Emily.' She smiled. 'I'm feeling a bit…'

He lunged as she collapsed, trying to prevent her from falling heavily. He managed to catch her upper body, stop her head striking the ground. He was on the floor, kneeling beside her.

'Rose – Emily – are you alright?' he said.

He'd thought she'd fainted, but her eyes were still open, gazing at his. Her startling eyes, like a wild, green sea, untamed, on the far side of the world.

'You're a good boy,' she said. 'Not like him. It's just… I don't do good boys.'

He closed his eyes, trying to contain his swimming emotion. He wanted to kiss her, kiss those broad, beautiful lips but – no. She was in love with her ex-husband, the poet. *And she was a killer.* A murderer.

'What have you done?' he said.

'He never changed them.'

'What?'

'The locks, here at Ashcraig. Before returning the keys, I had a set cut.'

He was starting to form a picture of events in his mind. He remembered the journal entry of the girl, it was a day out, wasn't it? They went to Glasgow on the 22nd – so they would have been back on the 23rd, today, no, today was Christmas Eve, so – *yesterday…*

'You were here when they came back?' he said.

She nodded. 'I hid a video camera near the gates – one of those cheap things off Amazon – so knew when they were in or out. Not that I needed it – the Christmas trip to Glasgow was a family tradition, even in my day.' She smiled. 'You are a beautiful boy,' she added.

He felt irked, the way she kept calling him a boy. And shamed by his continuing desire.

'So how did you get here?' She couldn't drive, after all, he thought. Unless…

'My car's parked in a layby further on, near the brook.'

'We could have escaped!'

She looked at him. 'I left you, to finish clearing up. I hoped you'd go before…'

'So… you lied?' All that wasted time, searching for keys. They could have left any time. 'How did you… how…?' he could barely bring himself to say it. 'How did you do it?' It was clear from the absence of blood she hadn't used the gun.

'Glycol. In the drinks. The mixers, Coke, tonic, squash. Even the cough syrup. Covered everything they might drink when they got back. It's sweet, you see, doesn't taste. They all had it.'

Ryan's head reeled. He thought of the brown splashes in the sink, the girl in the gallery, vomiting. He remembered Connie's book, the reference to ectoplasm, to the *fresh* dead. The black stuff… Was it because they'd only just died? 'But they would have called for help, as they began to get ill…' he said.

'It wasn't the snow brought down the line and Wi-Fi,' she said.

'You did it,' he whispered.

86.

'It's easy enough, when you know how,' she said. 'I have all the electrician qualifications for my work in the theatre, in lighting.'

Ryan was thinking. 'But poison – no poison kills immediately? Surely…'

'I shot him when he was trying to get them in the car. He died screaming on the ground. The bastard. I wanted to make sure he knew it was me. I stood on his chest, looked him in the eyes as I shot him again. The others scattered. Georgina collapsed in the gallery upstairs, Harry made it out into the fields, Emily even further up the road, but I brought them back in my car, Coran…'

She stopped, as if she'd surprised herself with the abject horror of her words, her explanation. They remained silent for a moment, struggling with the incomprehensible. Ryan thought about the stains by the Range Rover, ectoplasm, surely – he would never forget that reek now – but blood, maybe, too…

Then, remembering who and where he was, he laid her down and stood up, strode quickly towards the hidden closet.

'What are you doing?' she said, lifting herself up on her elbow.

He ignored her, ducked down into the darkness and said: 'You're OK – I'm here to help!'

The boy was weak, impossibly weak, so he had to pull him away, out from the tangled limbs of his own family, back into the open.

'You're OK, you'll be OK,' he was saying, pushing back the damp hair from his clammy forehead. How old was he? Five? Six? His skin was grey and he was breathing in shallow, interrupted breaths. His eyes were open, just a little. 'You're a brave boy, such a brave boy...'

Something else was happening to Ryan now, something boiling up from his guts.

Anger. Fury.

Still kneeling by the boy, trying to make him comfortable, he twisted around towards Rose - *Emily*. 'Get the bloody phones back on and call an ambulance!' he shouted.

There was no response.

'Call the ambulance!' he said again.

He realised she had turned her face to the floor and was sobbing.

'For God's sake, call the bloody ambulance!' He had to fight his confusion, get beyond his anger. He was going to have to call them himself, work out what she'd done to disconnect the service. He pressed the boy's jaw down, checked his mouth was clear, then eased him over on to his front, into the recovery position. Turned to stand but then cowered at once, seeing Emily above him with the barrel of the gun in her hands, the butt raised high over her head.

87.

'No!' he screamed, raising his arm to defend himself.

Too late to get up or dive away, he ducked his head, anticipating the full force of a deadly blow.

Nothing came.

Or rather, he felt something, a wetness, splash against the back of his head. A foul smell, reek.

He looked up.

Above him, around him, was a maelstrom of hashed obsidian, the seething Black, and spirits breaking through, two, three, four, the man, woman, boy and teenage girl, all screeching, shattering the peace of the library with their rage, with fury and terror, hands and necks stretching out towards the woman, Emily, her face distorted with panic and incomprehension as she staggered back, back towards the hearth, the Old Man of the Black's furrowed face screaming at her, the woman's mouth wide open, stretched with hatred, making that terrible shriek, the kids shaking and screeching, adding to the horrific cacophony…

Emily's heel clipped the edge of the hearth and she tumbled back, hitting her head on the mantelpiece and slumping into the fire.

Moments later, she was ablaze, crumpled on the hearth.

V.

New Year's Day

88.

He pulled the Toyota up in front of the building and turned off the engine.

Listened to the ticking. Looked up at the modern, brown-brick block, ahead in the snow.

Ryan took a deep breath, picked up the flowers from the passenger seat, opened the door and climbed out of the cabin. The backs of his thighs were still sore, but the padding of the bandages made it sufferable. They had dug all the pellets out one by one, over the course of an hour. He hardly felt the bitter chill as he walked to the building, past the entry sign on poles, into the heated foyer.

Behind the glass counter, a lean, middle-aged man in a checked shirt looked up at him through black-rimmed glasses.

'I've come to see my sister,' he said. 'Isla Harris.'

89.

He took the old lilies out of the enamel vase and replaced them with the new. Their rich pinky-cream provided a splash of vibrancy to the dull white décor of the room.

'There you go, sis,' he said. 'New flowers. For New Year.'

He pulled the yellow plastic armchair closer to the bed and perched beside her. He took hold of her hand. Studied her face, the delicate moons of her closed eyelids. As usual, imagined the slight flicker of movement.

He didn't know what to say. Things went through his head. He pushed them away.

'It wasn't much of a Christmas,' he said. After a moment he laughed. 'Jeez…' he added.

He looked at her face, turned away from him, to the side. Thankfully, she could breathe unaided, didn't need the apparatus some of them had. He saw those others through the windows, every time he came up to her floor.

Her mouth was closed, her bob long grown out so her hair was tangled, damp and dark against her neck. She was wearing a cotton gown with a soft collar around the throat. Breathing gently through her nose. She looked, as ever, like she was asleep. Like when they were kids and she was in the bed beside his, their father belting out a pretty good version of *All the Young Dudes* downstairs as he prepared a late-night fry-up in the kitchen. How did she ever get to sleep through that?

'She was driven mad by it,' he said at last.

He noticed a buzzing sound. Was that a fly in the middle of winter? It was, he saw it settle by the family picture he'd put on her table, all of them tanned in their swimmers in Guernsey, all grinning except his mum who was looking off to the left, distracted by something. It was a helicopter, he thought, recalling the detail for the first time. He stood, swatted the fly easily and wiped it against his jeans.

'Can't have that landing on you, can we, sis?' he said, sitting back down. He took her limp hand in his again.

He looked at the drip, the odd gaps here and there in the tube, the only evidence of the liquid feed running into her other hand.

'Love,' he said. 'What a bastard, eh? But I guess she must have been mad anyway. What would the world be like if we all killed for unreturned love?'

He thought about her face then, the white skin, those broad, full lips, creased. Her eyes beneath his, reflecting the firelight, green with tiny flecks, lost amid those mesmerising black stars...

Most of what she'd told him was a lie, of course, complete fabrication, all that stuff about the bean nighe, the ghost in the library, perhaps most of the history of Ashcraig... She was a consummate liar in fact, had a real talent for it.

And yet, he couldn't stop thinking about her.

'Now I'm going to cry,' he said. He reached up with his free hand and wiped his eyes, at the corner, one after the other.

'Anyway, you don't need me to tell you, do you, sis? That she got in that house and poisoned their drinks while they were away, hid until they were all dead – or dying. Only the youngest, Coran, somehow survived it, the dose he had was enough to make him unconscious for a while, but not kill him. He's making a good recovery, has some uncles and aunts, cousins looking after him. He was lucky. The fires had all been built up, there were a few petrol cans in the car port the Inspector thinks she brought in while I was asleep. He reckons she was planning to burn the whole place down…'

He gazed up at the white ceiling through blurred eyes, trying to see where it ended against the wall in the muted daylight. There was a plastic Christmas tree with tiny baubles on the windowsill, the staff must have put it there. Maybe that nice nurse, Felicity, the one who was always offering him a mint.

'But those ghosts, sis,' he said. 'The ghosts of them, the family…' He saw Emily's face, screaming at him as it materialised in front of her portrait, Peter's prematurely aged face shouting at him in the carport.

'So angry, but who wouldn't be?' he said. 'Not at me, just at… being dead. Their lives stolen from them, too early.' He took a deep breath. 'And thank you, thank you so much, sis. For what you did. For helping me, like that.'

Silence. He listened. Now he noticed it, it was complete. No sounds like you'd expect, no footsteps in the corridor, doors banging, vehicles reversing outside. It was quiet. It helped him think.

Yes, he remembered now – or rather half-remembered, through a kind of sense-impression. Could you have half a memory? He thought you could. When they were young, probably just before their teens, he'd been daydreaming on the sofa, the TV on, some sitcom, he wasn't really paying attention, couldn't even remember what it was called…

And there had been a taste in his mouth, sharp, sweet, delicious. Summer fruit. It was baking inside and out, the hottest day of the year. He smiled at the flavour, felt his mouth watering, swallowed.

And then the rattle of the key, creaking of the front door as it opened and shut. She came into the doorway of the lounge and stood there, in her white school shirt and grey skirt. His sister.

Chewing, with a punnet of strawberries in her hand.

90.

'Mr Harris…'

He looked up, surprised to find himself there, in the room, still holding Isla's hand. He must have been daydreaming, or possibly asleep? He turned to see the nurse behind him, a woman with a thin neck, red lipstick and wispy blonde hair that he guessed was dyed.

'Sorry, I was lost in my own little world.'

She smiled kindly at him. 'No problem. But we're five minutes past the end of visiting time.'

'I'll be on my way.'

Her grey eyes shone with care, as she turned and disappeared back through the door.

Ryan stood and leaned over his sister, pecked her on the cheek. 'I won't be able to come tomorrow, sis,' he said. 'I've got a load of orders in, and the grand-sounding D.I. Lazenfort is coming to see me. Lazenfort.' he repeated, and chuckled. 'They're always after more detail, not surprising, I suppose. But I'll be back the day after.'

He walked out slowly, almost backwards, watching carefully her motionless eyelids.

91.

The first thing he noticed as he came out the building were the deep grey clouds bearing down on the horizon – another storm brewing, for sure.

He checked his watch, realised he'd been in there nearly two hours. It would soon be dark. What was he going to do this evening? Rob had asked him over to his folk's house, they were cooking beef wellington and having a few people over. Rich and Susy Fenton liked to do something on New Year's Day, it was a bit of a tradition. He got on well with Rob's parents, Susy had been a travelling saleswoman in the days before mobiles and the internet took over and she was a right laugh. But he didn't think he could cope with it now. Too intense. He didn't know how he'd react to people pussyfooting around him. Probably best just to stay in, watch a film on his own.

He was moving towards the van when he heard a bleep, someone else in the carpark, unlocking their car. He turned and saw a woman, standing by a silver SUV.

He froze.

There was something about her, the way she stood, even though she was wrapped in a long red coat, something about her figure, the way she held herself. And that hair, long, black, thick down her back, surely…

The woman turned into profile and he saw the shape of her face, her short, pointy nose and small chin.

It wasn't her. How could it be? She was dead.

But his heart had lurched. Not with fear, but hope. A desperate hope.

Despite her being a killer, a despicable *child* killer, he thought, standing there in the drizzle – now he knew there was no permanent separation between this world and the next – how would he ever be free?

And did he want to be?

Thank you for reading my book, I hope you enjoyed it!

If you did, I would be very grateful if you could post a rating or short review on Amazon or Goodreads. Your ratings make a real difference to authors, helping the books you enjoy reach more people.

Other Books by Steve Griffin

Black Beacon: A Christmas Ghost Story

1976. The South Downs.
The Christmas it snowed.
The Christmas that evil returned…

Struggling with money, Theo and Nat are doing their best to make Christmas special. It's been a hard time of year for them, ever since a family tragedy.

But this year, their troubles are just beginning. They are about to be visited by a terrifying ghost from Christmas past, a spirit that will bring back not just the horror of the war that divided them but also a deep, hidden betrayal from their early life together…

Will Theo and Nat survive the haunting and wounds of their past?

Read on for an excerpt from Black Beacon:

The Tree

Theo

Theo sat in his Beetle, waiting for twilight so he could steal the tree.

Elbows on the large steering wheel, he watched the hills for labourers, perhaps a lone herdsman from Mr Wolfson's farm bringing the cattle home for the night over the Beacon, or a farmhand returning to Friston with his shoulder pack of tools.

There was no one. Just the light silvering on the horizon as darkness descended from the tallest parts of the sky.

It was cold. The warmth from the fan heater, never very effective, had dissipated within minutes of switching off the engine. Theo sat back and rubbed his hands on his nylon trousers then fished his tobacco tin out from his pocket. He found the papers on the dashboard, prised open the Old Holborn, and pinched a few moist strands from the tin. The tobacco smelt strong, sharp, almost vinegary. A smell he loved. Theo stretched the baccy along the paper, rolled and lifted it to his lips for licking. Pinched it over, sealed it.

The light from the struck match brightened the cabin, making Theo realise it was sufficiently dark to move ahead with his plan.

He opened the door and stepped out into the bitter December chill. He stuck his fag in his mouth and pulled his sheepskin coat tight around him, wrestling the large buttons into their infuriatingly tight holes. Then lifted the driver seat forward and took the handsaw out from the back.

One last check up the hillside, down along the track he'd come in on.

Not a living thing. No man, cow, nor sheep, not even a lonely gull adrift in the sky. He was alone.

The end of his fag blazed as he inhaled.

Theo blew smoke from the corner of his mouth as he turned and ambled towards the wood, clutching his saw.

*

When he entered the trees he wished he'd scouted for a good specimen in daylight.

The remaining brightness faded with every few steps, crowded out by the sturdy trunks of elms not yet touched by disease, by slender oaks and the black skeletal branches of birch, such a contrast to their peeling white bark. Theo knew the Forestry Commission managed this old pocket of wood, some of it ancient, some of it new plantation. He'd seen from the brow of the Beacon that part of the plantation had been cleared a few years ago and was now surging with new growth. That was where he was headed now.

But God, he thought, he never expected it to get this dark this quickly. The mist from his breath was scarcely visible, but he could feel the warm ghost of it round his cheeks. With a final deep draw to the back of his lungs, he flicked away the small ember of his rollie.

The snap of the undergrowth beneath his boots increased as the wood grew greyer, more gloomy. Theo felt a momentary despondency, such as he'd not felt in years. Why was he doing this? He heard a ringing sound in his ears, aggressive and high pitched, the old tinnitus coming back. Like a wasp.

He thought of Nat, the sweet way she smiled, with the lines at the corner of her mouth. The worry lines.

That was why. He was going to make her Christmas. This year, they were going to have a good one.

He would make sure of that.

*

Dark shapes all around. A fuzzy hint of light overhead, barely penetrating the forest floor, the spidery duff on which he stood.

But at least he'd found his tree.

Theo knelt and felt around the thin, rough twigs at the base of the pine. There wasn't much space to get the saw in, make a clean cut. But this was surely it, a six-footer he wouldn't struggle to get in the back of the car. Something that would bring the living room to life, standing proud in the bay window. He imagined it all aglow with fairy lights. Nat might even like to buy a few baubles, some gold and silver tinsel, too. He'd saved a couple of quid on the tree, they would have enough for a few cheap decorations. They'd always scrimped on a tree before. With just the two of them alone in Black Beacon it had seemed an unnecessary – and a pricey – extravagance. He was sure it would cheer her up. Nat needed cheering up.

'*Verdammt!*' he cried, as the saw jammed in the damp wood. With no one around, he surprised himself, slipping back into German. Except for the odd *scheisse*, he hadn't done that in years.

He set to again, elbow pistoning back and forth. Stopped, wiping away sweat. This was harder than he'd thought.

Another fevered saw, then he paused, hacking phlegm from the top of his lungs. There was some pain in there. Ach, the damned fags…

Something called out in the forest, pretty much in the dark now. It was a bird, he thought. Not a crow, not raw or harsh like that. A more whooping sound. He didn't know his birds.

More sawing. Feeling in amid the denser, higher branches with his free hand, he found the trunk. The thing was starting to yield, he could relieve the pressure on the blade by pushing hard. He did that. A few frenzied hacks later and he was through, there was a slow crack and the tree fell, softly rolling on its coat of needles across the ground.

Theo stood and wiped his brow with the sleeve of his padded coat. He stooped and lifted the tree up by the cut end. It was quite heavy, and he couldn't use both hands because of the saw. He let go, eased his fingers through the prickly branches to find a balance point. Then lifted it again, and looked around.

It was dark. Dark and cold.

He wished he'd brought his torch. But he knew his way back, so it wasn't essential. He started to walk, holding the tree away from the ground. He didn't want to lose any needles.

*

An owl *hoo-hooed* amid the dark blocks of trees. He was having increasing trouble avoiding stumbling into trunks. There was still a little light bringing out shadows, helping him avoid the worst collisions. And the bulk of the tree was slowing and steadying him, so if he did happen to hit or trip on something, it wasn't hard to correct himself.

But... he thought he should be out of the forest by now.

He was back in the deciduous area, traipsing through a leafy mulch instead of pine duff. But he had been expecting to see the break in the trees for a few minutes now and there was only... the darkness of more trees crowding in.

Theo didn't have a good sense of direction, not like a man was supposed to. Not that Nat's was any better, they used to joke that the pair of them could get lost between the pub and the car. Never drink and drive, Nat would say. Wouldn't dream of it, he'd reply, I finished my pint in the pub!

But now he was feeling it, that shadow of hopelessness that came from not knowing, not being sure of where he was going. It was bloody freezing out here, he didn't want to be out for much longer.

He came into a small grassy clearing and stopped. He hadn't been here before. He looked up at the sky, deep purple now, the evening star visible to his right. It came out over the Channel, didn't it? Which meant he should bear left. The track with the car was on the, what would it be? – the east side of the wood, away from the sea.

He turned to face the knot of trees and was about to take a step when something moved in the corner of his eye.

Theo stopped and looked around.

There was someone there. Someone standing in the trees to his right.

'Hello there, man!' he shouted. 'You!'

The figure, just a dark shape, remained still. He was a half a dozen or so yards back in the trees, facing Theo. A woodsman?

'Hello,' he called again. He took a step towards the man. 'I think I… I'm not sure where my car is…' He looked down, embarrassed by the tree in his hand. Would it be obvious what he'd been doing? If he was a forester, might he get fined for something like this?

But the man wasn't responding. Theo must be wrong. It was just another tree trunk, surely, perhaps snapped by lightning?

He had that feeling of deflation again, like he'd had upon entering the woods. What was he doing? A grown man, stealing a tree he could afford… Even though their finances were particularly squeezed at the moment, there were those much poorer than him. In McFadden's, the bakery where he worked, there was Jonesy for instance, with four young boys to feed on less than twenty quid a week. And Mary, with her husband on the permanent sick. How did they make ends meet?

What was the point of this?

Theo glanced at the tree, then back at the shape. The shape moved.

'Hey...' said Theo.

The man appeared to gesture with an arm. Then he turned and walked away, deeper into the woods.

'Aye, aye, aye,' Theo muttered. He felt strangely spooked. Maybe the man was mute or something, couldn't speak? Was he trying to show Theo the way?

Come on, he thought, feeling things, his brightness of spirit, draining away, as if into the damp ground. To follow, or not to follow?

He followed.

The Ghosts of Alice

The Ghosts of Alice is a series of standalone ghost stories featuring Alice Deaton, a young woman with a mysterious connection to the dead.

The Boy in the Burgundy Hood

** THE #1 INTERNATIONAL BESTSELLER **

Will it be her dream job – or a waking nightmare?

Alice can't believe her luck when she lands a new post at a medieval English manor house. Mired in debt, the elderly owners have transferred their beloved Bramley to a heritage trust. Alice must prepare it for opening to the public, with the former owners relegated to a private wing.

But when the ghosts start appearing – the woman with the wounded hand and the boy in the burgundy hood – Alice realises why her predecessor might have left the isolated house so soon. As she peels back the layers of the mystery, the secrets Alice uncovers haunting Bramley's heart will be dark – darker than she could ever have imagined…

The Girl in the Ivory Dress

Will a strange request help her move on from a haunted past?

After a fire tears through the country house where she works, Alice accepts a desperate invitation from a friend whose guest house is being haunted.

But when Alice arrives at the remote Peacehaven, she senses something much stranger going on. Who is the ghastly spectre roaming the house? Why is he terrifying the guests? And why does Alice keep dreaming about the ghosts of her past, the burning man and girl in the ivory dress?

As she digs deeper, Alice will uncover an insidious evil that might just overwhelm her...

Alice and the Devil

'Yes, I can see ghosts,' she said.
'That's why she told me to come here. Because you can help us. You can help grandad and me. You can help us defeat him.'
'Him?'
'Yes, him. The Devil.'

A boy crosses the moors in a storm to plead for Alice's help, claiming to be sent by a ghost.

Is the boy's grandfather really being terrorised by the Devil himself? Alice can't believe it – but then she's experienced things she'd never imagined could come true. But even with her paranormal experiences, little does she expect the horror she is about to face at the lonely rectory overlooking the moors…

Other books in The Ghosts of Alice series:

Alice and the Broken Dead

The Woman in the Widow's Lace

Psychological Thriller

The Man in the Woods

Who is the Man in the Woods?

The woods are deep and dark and cold and empty…
… except for a solitary boy, out riding his bike…
… and a lone wanderer…
What will happen when their paths cross?

Whatever it is, things will never be the same again.

The Man in the Woods is a chilling standalone thriller with a dark twist.

About the Author

Steve Griffin is the author of seventeen books, known for his supernatural thrillers full of twists and turns including the bestselling Ghosts of Alice series and his Christmas ghost stories.

Steve has also written a fast-paced mystery adventure series for young adults, The Secret of the Tirthas. A Guardian review of the first book, The City of Light, calls it 'entertaining and exciting.'

Steve loves exploring the Surrey Hills, where he lives with his wife and two sons. He enjoys a good indie gig and is a lifelong fan of horror movies.

To keep updated on his writing, hit the follow button on Amazon or sign up to his newsletter by emailing stevegriffin.author@outlook.com. You can also check out his website at steve-griffin.com or follow him on Instagram and Facebook – @stevegriffin.author.

Printed in Dunstable, United Kingdom